Just A Bet

A Sweet Holiday Romantic Comedy

Copyright © 2021 Jenessa Fayeth

All rights reserved

The characters and events portrayed in this book are fictitious. Any similarity to real persons, living or dead, is coincidental and not intended by the author.

No part of this book may be reproduced, or stored in a retrieval system, or transmitted in any form or by any means, electronic, mechanical, photocopying, recording, or otherwise, without express written permission of the publisher.

ISBN-13: 9798778471641

Editor: Jill Burrell
Cover design by: Jenessa Fayeth
Library of Congress Control Number: 2018675309
Printed in the United States of America

*Dedicated to Brynlee,
and all the little sisters to brothers out there.*

Contents

Title Page
Copyright
Dedication

The Problem:	1
Chapter 1	2
The Solution:	8
Chapter 2	9
Chapter 3	16
Chapter 4	21
Chapter 5	28
Chapter 6	34
Chapter 7	38
Chapter 8	47
Chapter 9	54
Chapter 10	61
Chapter 11	67
Chapter 12	73
Chapter 13	78

Chapter 14	89
Chapter 15	98
Chapter 16	105
Chapter 17	112
Chapter 18	115
Chapter 19	123
Chapter 20	127
Chapter 21	133
Chapter 22	137
Chapter 23	141
Chapter 24	150
Epilogue	157
Thank you!	161
Wait!	163
Acknowledgements	165
About The Author	167
Books In This Series	169
Books By This Author	171

The Problem:

My brothers

Chapter 1

Lennox

Six years ago

My brothers are making bets again.

I knew before I came on this date. My first date, to be exact. Now I'm standing on the front porch under the dim light with Lucas Shaw, waiting for him to kiss me, yet terrified he'll actually do it. Because we have an audience.

He doesn't know that, of course.

But I do. The light on the video doorbell keeps flickering and I can almost see their eager faces hovering over a phone screen.

Michael a senior, will try to get everyone to up their bets because he always needs more gas money. The twins, Trent and Sean, are juniors and will fight over who made the correct bet first. And Grant, Trent and Sean's best friend, will just be watching, patiently waiting, ready to laugh at the outcome.

Will he like the outcome tonight? Or will he be jealous? I'd like him to be?

Shivers race down my spine, and I take a step away from Lucas. I should probably let him down now. It will be easier that way.

"I had a really great time tonight." I smile. I'd been crushing on Lucas since he drew a self-portrait in our freshman art class a month ago. It was an eagle engulfed in flames. Obviously, it was completely symbolic and perfect.

"Me too." Lucas swipes his long black bangs back from his face and takes a step closer.

Oh no. He's going to do it.

And I *really* want him to. But he can't. Not here.

"You want to take a walk?" I blurt.

His eyebrows furrow. "Sure."

I grab his hand before he can change his mind and start walking down the street. There is a little park with a gazebo four houses down. I've dreamt of having my first kiss there for years. Usually, I'm picturing a different guy, but Lucas has all my attention now.

"I was super nervous to ask you out," Lucas says as we pass the first house.

I look up to see if he's kidding. "Really? Why?" He's the only guy who has even flirted with me this year. Every other guy I'm interested in practically runs the other direction.

He lifts his shoulder, then drops it. "Your brothers are kind of intimidating."

I study the porch railing of the next house. "They're harmless." The biggest lie I've ever told in my life.

"I know that now." His thumb rubs the back of my hand and tingles shoot up my arm. "Having three big brothers probably makes dating difficult."

Try impossible. He's forgetting Grant. He practically lives at our house and is just as annoying as the other three.

"Ha. Yeah." I swallow. I wasn't about to admit this was my first date and my brothers had all freaked when I told them.

Michael had wanted to know what we were doing, probably so they could all spy on me. Thankfully, none of them were in the back of the theater when Lucas had put his arm around my shoulders. I know this solely based on the fact that he still has two arms, and that one wasn't ripped from his body by four wannabe bodybuilders. Only one of them has muscles worth mentioning or appreciating. And thankfully, we do not share the same last name.

Enough about my brothers and Grant. This is my first kiss.

That thought doesn't calm my nerves. Do I really want my first kiss to be with Lucas?

The park is only one house away now, and I fight everything in me to not pull my hand back and wipe my clammy palms on my jeans.

What am I supposed to do with my lips when he kisses me? Oh gosh. My armpits are sweaty. What if I'm a terrible kisser and he tells everyone at school?

We reach the gazebo and I freeze despite the warm Phoenix night. The butterflies in my stomach have turned to ping pongs, ricocheting around and I think I'm going to be sick. Is this what everyone feels like before their first kiss?

Lucas looks down at me with a gentle smile. "You're so pretty."

That's the line. The one right before the kiss. And I don't believe it for a second.

"Thanks," I barely manage to say.

His fingers tighten around mine, and his other hand comes up to my chin.

This is it. This is where I have my first kiss. Or maybe have a heart attack. My breathing speeds up, and he smiles because he knows what he's doing to me.

But he doesn't really.

Unless his goal is to make me hyperventilate.

"Lennox!" Four voices pierce through the calm evening air.

The ping pong balls turn to bowling balls and my stomach bottoms out. "Oh no."

"Is that—" Lucas swallows.

"We saw some creeper pulling you into the dark, and we called the cops. Where are you?" Michael calls.

Lucas jumps away from me and shoots me a terrified look. My embarrassment evaporates and all that's left is the raging fire inside of me.

I hate my brothers.

"Lennox. There you are!" Grant and my brothers crowd around me until I can't see Lucas anymore.

I glare at each of them. "What are you doing?"

"Saving your life," says Sean, my middle and most annoying brother.

"I think I better go." Lucas's voice is barely audible, and I know he's already walking away. Nothing could make him stay.

Everything feels so far away. I can see my brother's faces and hear their voices, but I'm afraid if I move, I'll strangle one of them.

"Why would you come out here in the dark?" Michael asks.

"Because I can never escape you!" Four equally stunned faces stare back at me like I've lost it. Maybe I have. "I'll never, ever bring another guy home as long as you guys live here. And I'll never date as long as you're around."

My brothers wear matching expressions of amusement, but Grant has the audacity to look sorry for me.

"Good," Trent says. "Told you she'd get pissed. You guys owe me fifteen bucks."

"No, you said she'd slap the guy." Sean corrects him, and my brothers leave, fighting over who won the actual bet.

It was just a bet. Everything is always a bet to them. Never mind that they just ruined my first date. One of them won some extra spending money, and that's all that matters.

I drop my head. Anger and humiliation fight for room in my heart, but tears are all that escape.

"I'm sorry, Len," Grant whispers.

Heat floods my veins, and I glare up at him. "I don't need your pity."

He flinches, and I instantly regret snapping at him. I'm sure he gets enough of that at home from his father.

He drops his head. "I tried to talk them out of coming but they never listen to me."

"Bull. They listen to you more than me."

He avoids my eyes and shoves a hand through his curly black hair. "They were just saving you from a horrible first kiss."

My heart gives a funny flip hearing him say the word kiss. I can't help it. This is the boy I've always pictured my first kiss with. He is two years older than me, the same age as the twins. He's quiet and reserved at school, but I've seen his fun and energetic side. The side that if other girls saw, he'd never be available. But he's not available to me, anyway; I'm basically his little sister.

My mouth drops open. "It wasn't going to be horrible!"

He lifts his left eyebrow, the one with a scar through it that makes him look dangerous and exciting.

"Really? Because you looked miserable."

He wasn't wrong. "Because I knew you and my brothers were going to ruin it. Just like everything else!"

Grant's eyes soften. "Your first kiss shouldn't scare you." His voice is deeper than any of the guys my age, and that is the only reason I shiver.

I snort, but it sounds more like I'm choking. "You thought I was scared?"

He takes a step closer and my breathing speeds up by default. "You were terrified to kiss him."

Who was I afraid to kiss? Oh, Lucas. Only Lucas.

"You were two seconds from puking," Grant says.

I hate that he's right. I also hate that he's standing so close I can't think of a good comeback.

"So I think the words you're looking for now are 'thank you'." He smiles confidently and dang it if confidence doesn't look amazing on him, just like everything else.

I take a deep breath and come back to my senses. He may be the boy I can't get off my mind night and day, but he just wrecked my first kiss. "I don't need you or anyone else saving me from a kiss. I'll make sure you aren't around for my next one."

His dark eyes harden ever so slightly. "We'll see about that."

The Solution:

A fake engagement

Lennox

Six years later

I look at the drawing on my computer screen. It's so boring. Nothing but cabinets, cabinets, and more cabinets. I switch tabs and I'm back to my favorite illustration app. I never wanted to work at the family cabinet shop. But six months ago, I decided it was time to stop mooching off my parents. I know how blessed I've been to have supportive parents, which is why I'm determined to prove I can take what they've taught me and make something of myself. I'll be graduating after spring semester and then I have to figure out my life. Which conveniently starts in the one place I've been avoiding for the last twenty-one years, working at my family's cabinet shop.

Speaking of, I should get back to the actual work on my plate: drawing the jobs for my dad. I switch screens and glance at the clock. I have only fifteen minutes to finish designing this job before I need to head to class. Which I can do as long as no one bugs me—

"It wasn't half bad. I think I might get a pedicure again." Sean says and my other two brothers laugh as they burst into my office.

Well, it was a nice thought.

"Nope." I point a finger at them to leave, but they're

oblivious.

"I can't believe you went through with it," Michael says with a shake of his head.

"I can. It's Sean," says Trent, "He doesn't need a bet to act like a girl."

Sean throws an arm around Trent's neck and they bump into my desk, knocking a stack of business cards to the floor.

"Would you please get out of my office?" I try to intervene before they send my computer flying.

They stop fighting and lean over my desk in unison.

"What do you want?" I eye them skeptically. They're each handsome in their own way, but no two are similar, not even the twins. Michael and I are the only ones with blond hair. The twins both have brown hair, but that's where their similarities end. Sean has light brown eyes like me and Trent has blue like Michael.

"Nothing." Trent shrugs and steals a chocolate from the bowl on my desk. "Dad told us to meet him here."

"Well, since you're here, can we please talk about the beards? They need to go. It's December." I say. I've sat through way too many No Shave November family dinners, watching food crumbs tumble from those birds' nests and I can't do it anymore.

"I can't." Trent says. He's right. He has a total baby face without a beard, but the other two don't have the same excuse.

"At least trim it." I sigh and try to focus on my plans again. "You look like cavemen."

"Why do you get an office and we don't?" Michael asks for the fiftieth time since I came to work at the shop. As the oldest, he has been working with dad the longest and is currently the foreman.

I understand why he's upset. I also don't care.

"Because I'm the favorite," I say, my voice heavy with sarcasm. It isn't an office. It's a glorified closet with a desk and computer. But somehow, it's always the most packed place in the shop because of these fools right here.

"I don't pick favorites," Dad says, sliding into the room. He winks and kisses me on the forehead.

"I'm glad you're all here. I'm looking into dates for the Christmas work party. Does anyone have conflicts with the seventeenth?" Dad looks around.

"I do." Sean says.

Great. I'm never getting out of here.

We spend the next five minutes discussing dates and times, finally narrowing down the perfect date.

"Hey guys. What are we talking about?" Says a deep voice from my doorway. This voice doesn't set me on edge like my brothers' voices do. It's deep and warm and gets my heart racing every time I hear it.

Grant.

"Great. Now it's a party." I mutter, though my insides do a little happy dance.

Because my crush on him still hasn't died. It's only gotten bigger and stronger, just like his biceps. The last couple years have been exceptionally good to him, probably because he runs the installation crew, so he spends his days lifting heavy cabinets with those tree trunks called arms.

I've wasted way too much time thinking about him doing that job shirtless. But he can never know. Neither can anyone else, for that matter. Hence, the reason I pretend he's just one of my brothers.

"We're discussing the holiday party. How's the twenty-second?" My dad asks him.

Grant nods without bothering to check his calendar. "That works."

"Are we bringing dates this year?" Trent asks.

The guys all snort.

"I don't know if we should after last year." Dad glares at Sean.

Sean's hands shoot in the air. "I didn't know she was a belly dancer. Or that she was going to give everyone a show."

I laugh along with the guys, even though I wasn't there. I've heard so many versions, and know everyone was uncomfortable during that unprecedented performance, but no one was more uncomfortable than Sean because halfway through her routine, she managed to get him shaking his hips along with her. Thank goodness Michael got a video. We watch it at least once a month at our family dinner.

"It wasn't a show. It was a nightmare," Trent exaggerates.

"We can't help it if Sean likes the nightmares," Michael chuckles.

Sean tries to put Michael in a headlock, but Michael jumps behind my chair, squishing me into my desk.

"You can bring a date," Dad says. "But I think I'd like to meet her first."

Sean scoffs. "Why just my date? Why not Michael's?"

"Because Michael's date better be his fiancée," Dad says with a chuckle. "But it goes for everyone else. You too Lennox."

My head shoots up, and five pairs of eyes stare back at me.

"W-what?"

"Ha! Like little Lenny would dare bring a date to the work Christmas party." Sean says with a laugh. I want to agree with him. I know how out of hand the holiday party tends to get, but I also hate when he's right.

"Sure I would." I shrug like it's no big deal, but inside I'm shaking. I haven't been on a date for... a long time.

"Should we make a bet?" Michael asks. He is always the first to suggest a bet.

I should have seen this coming. "No." I'm so over their stupid games.

"Oh, come on. This is the best idea yet." Sean says, beaming.

"I'm out of here," Dad says. "Good luck, sweetie."

"Dad?" I groan, but he's already gone.

"We probably shouldn't gamble on Lennox's love life anymore." Grant speaks up and something akin to hope rises in my chest.

I look at him, fully appreciating his handsome features. If he's my knight in shining armor, I'm throwing down my hair, puckering my lips, whatever it takes to ride off into the sunset with him.

"But we're still going to." Michael says, and Grant smirks.

My eyes narrow. I'd hoped after high school that he would finally see me as more than a little sister, but no such luck.

"How about we make this bet more interesting?" Michael says.

I already hate where this is going. I flick off my monitor and stand up. The drawing will have to wait until tomorrow. They'll make the bet with or without me here.

"I'll give you a hundred bucks to bring a guy to the holiday party," Michael says.

I freeze. "Me?" Usually, they just wager with each other over me.

"Yeah. I know you want to get out of mom and dad's house after graduation. So I'll contribute to your savings fund, or if all goes well, your wedding fund," Michael says, pumping his eyebrows.

My eyes widen. "What?" I'm not looking to get married. Sure, I've thought about it a few times. Like every time Grant walks into my office. I also may have added fifteen wedding dresses to my favorite Pinterest board yesterday, but I'll never admit that out loud.

"We'll each give you a hundred," Trent says.

"I never agreed to that." Grant steps back and folds his arms.

I look at him. His hat is backward and there's dust all over him, making his black hair look more brown, but he's just as sexy as he's ever been. And just as untouchable. I need to get over him, and the solution is right in front of me. Get a date.

"Everyone pays, or I don't do it." I plant my hands on my hips, ready for a stare-down if necessary.

Grant's lips quirk because he can never keep a straight face. That, or I look ridiculous.

"Fine. But if he's a loser, I reserve the right to kick him out of the party," Grant says finally.

"Agreed," Sean says.

"Absolutely not!" I jump in. "You can't just kick out my date because you don't like him. What if *I* like him?"

"You liked Lucas Shaw," Michael points out, giving me a condescending look, "I'm not sure you're the best judge of character."

My brothers laugh, and I shoot glares at them. Talk about beating a dead horse. "Fine. Get your wallets ready." Easiest four hundred bucks I'll ever make.

Chapter 3

Grant

Why am I as stubborn as Lennox's brothers? I don't want her to bring a date to the holiday party. I don't want her to ever date anyone unless it's me.

But she doesn't know this. Which is why I'm still making stupid wagers with her brothers about her love life.

No wonder she doesn't see me as anything more than a brother. I'm stuck and I don't know how to get rid of the facade I've been hiding behind for the last ten years.

I can't just tell my three best friends that I'm in love with their little sister and have been since we were in high school, threatening all the boys who even looked in her direction. They are the closest thing I have to a family, and if they reject me like they rejected every boy Lennox ever dated, I'd no longer have a place to call home, or a job.

My mom left when I was a baby, and my dad was an alcoholic who chose liquor over me. The only person I had was my grandfather until he passed away ten years ago. I can't survive a rejection from the Bentleys. They are all I have.

It's pathetic, I know. I've just been waiting, hoping some perfect opportunity will present itself and somehow Lennox will know my feelings for her.

I thought it almost happened a few months ago. We were the only two left in the shop when the alarm wigged out. We ended up locked together in the office for almost an hour.

At one point, right before the doors opened, she looked at me with her big doe eyes, and I swear she knew I'd been in love with her since high school.

I tried to tell her everything with my eyes. My feelings, my fears, my dreams. I almost leaned in to kiss her.

Then she asked me if I was constipated.

She may not reciprocate my feelings, but it doesn't stop me from visiting her whenever I can. If the alarm wigs out again, I want to be stuck with her.

If my grandpa was still here, he'd tell me I was a coward. That being in love is the bravest thing a man can be. I want to be brave.

I rub at my chest and the new tattoo above my heart that reminds me of him. I miss him so much.

"Dude, did you hear me?"

I pull out an earbud and turn to Michael. "Sorry, what?"

"I asked if you were good to go on the Whitney job?"

I shake my head free of my favorite obsession and run through my mental list again. "Still waiting on a corner piece from Sean."

"It's always Sean." Michael shakes his head and jots something down on his notepad. "How's Rick doing on the install team?"

"He only FaceTimes his girlfriend on his smoke break now." I say. Nevermind that he takes a smoke break every forty-five minutes. "He gets his job done." He at least does that. Most of the time.

"I guess that's progress. Keep him in line and you'll be the top installer by next year, I'm sure." Michael says, still writing on some plans. That sentence fills me with a sense of pride. I started working with Mark Bentley the day I turned sixteen, and I've loved every second. After my grandpa passed when I was fourteen, I jumped at every chance to avoid going home. Sports, work, the Bentley's home. Anything was better than what I had, which was a violent father. My grandfather shielded me from most of it when he could, and my aunt Megan tried to help as well, but there was only so much they could do.

Even after I graduated, I continued working at the shop. I couldn't afford university but I managed to pay my way through trade school, just like my grandpa had. He'd been a woodworker as well so the shop has always felt like home to me, and I couldn't imagine doing anything else.

"You coming to Trevor's tomorrow?" Michael asks, reminding me he's still there.

I shake my head. "Nah. I've got stuff to do at home." The word home almost makes me laugh, because it's barely four walls and a roof. I've saved every spare penny, and living in a tiny apartment in town helped with that, but I'm not ready to buy a new house yet. When I buy a house, I want to pay for it outright. Which is why I am willing to sacrifice for a little longer to achieve my dreams. It would help if I stopped making stupid bets with the Bentley brothers.

"You work too hard, man."

That's rich coming from the guy who used to work fifteen-hour days.

"Come have fun for once. Juliet is bringing a friend. She could be your date for the holiday party."

I clench my jaw. Again with this stupid party. Why did the brothers gamble on Lennox's dating life, anyway?

I thought they'd learned their lesson the first time. She gave us the silent treatment for a week after the Lucas incident. It hurt me the most. The guys just thought she was on her period or something.

"I don't think I'll bring a date," I admit. I'd rather have a good time than worry about what a stranger thinks of me and my friends. Plus, the work party is the worst place for a first date.

Something bad always happens. Last year it was Sean's belly dancer. The year before, the food made everyone sick. And the year before that, one employee got divorced, quite literally, over dinner.

"Is this because of the bet we made with Lennox?" Michael asks, and my eyes widen before I can stop them.

"What? No. This has nothing to do with Lennox."

Michael arches an eyebrow, and I turn to grab my tool belt. The workday is almost over, and I need to put it away before one of the newbies mistakes it for theirs again.

"Okay, if you say so," Michael says finally. "Don't forget about basketball tonight."

I snort, basketball gets me out of my lonely apartment, so does work and Sunday dinners with the Bentleys. I couldn't forget about it if I tried.

"I won't," I say, and head to the back of the shop.

I let out a breath. I dodged that bullet for now. But with my luck, not for long. Nothing good ever lasts. I learned that the first time my dad went to rehab after he'd thrown a beer bottle at my head. He'd promised me, while I was getting six stitches in my eyebrow, that he'd never hurt me again. Technically, he hasn't physically hurt me since then, but his absence hurts just as much as a needle to my face.

I haven't given up hope of good things in life. I'm just realistic now.

My phone rings, and I pull it from my pocket. Aunt Megan. The blood in my veins turns to ice. I should answer, but I can't. Every time my aunt calls, she begs me to build a bridge between my dad and I. Unfortunately, a bridge can't join two people who don't want to be connected anymore.

Chapter 4

Lennox

"He didn't." My almost sister-in-law Juliet groans loud enough that several people in the college library look over. Every little noise bounces off the plain white walls and floor to ceiling windows.

I duck my head behind my computer, pretending to study. Nothing to see here.

"He did," I whisper. "He made another stupid bet. At least I can get something out of it this time."

Juliet twists a strand of dark brown hair around her finger, a nervous tick she has. "I told Michael to stop. When is he ever going to grow up?"

I take off my blue-light glasses and clean them on my sleeve. "Try never. The Bentley breed is exceptionally immature."

"Maybe it's not the worst thing, though. You haven't dated in—"

"Yes, I know. Forever."

I'm still embarrassed about the night I got all chummy with Juliet and admitted to her that I've never even been kissed. That's right. I'm twenty-one and have never been kissed.

"So who are you going to bring?" Juliet asks. She unscrews the lid of her water bottle and takes a drink, draining the remainder. We've been sitting here for an hour and that's her second refill. No wonder she always has to pee.

"I don't know. It's not like I talk to guys a lot."

Okay, I never talk to guys.

And I can't even blame it all on my brothers and their obsession with butting into my life.

It's all me. After my train-wreck of an almost first kiss, I've only been on a handful of dates, and every time the kiss comes, I think about Grant's words. *"Your first kiss shouldn't scare you."* And then I get scared and have a mini panic attack.

"Well, he has to be hot, and preferably like six inches taller than your brothers, so they are intimidated by him," Juliet says while solving a math problem. How does she do that?

"I don't think Chris Hemsworth is available that night, but I'll ask." I roll my eyes.

She mimics my eye roll. "Just lie about what he does or something. Say he's saved a life, or that he's already a millionaire. Something that will make your brothers squirm."

"Ha!" I laugh. "The only guy that would make my brothers squirm is one I'm actually interested in."

Juliet drops her pencil and stares up at me as if she's just seen a ghost. "Oh, my gosh. That's it."

"What's it?"

"You should turn the tables on your brothers."

"That sounds great. But how?"

Juliet steeples her fingers together and gets a mischievous glint in her eye. "They think you won't dare show up with a date. Imagine what they'll do when you show up with your fiancé?"

"What?" I sputter, choking on air. "I don't have a fiancé."

Juliet's smile grows. "Not yet. But you will. We are going to find you a fake fiancé for the Christmas party."

"What? Huh? Fake?" My mouth doesn't seem to work any better than my mind.

"Yes." Juliet smiles and I discover a whole new side of my soon-to-be sister-in-law. "Introduce him as your date at the beginning of the night, then at the holiday party, you drop the bomb. That will teach them not to mess with your love life."

As much as I hate to admit it, her plan is kind of genius. My brothers and Grant would have a heart attack if I show up to the party engaged.

"But what about after? I won't marry a stranger for real."

Juliet snorts. "Of course not. I'd never let you do that."

"But you'll let me pretend to be engaged to one."

"Yes. Someone we know, of course." She clarifies. "For the cause. Those boys need to be taught a lesson. Imagine how awful they'll feel when you go through a terrible breakup. They will feel like it's all their fault when you're heartbroken, and they'll finally leave you alone."

I bite the end of my fingernail. "Do you really think that could work?" I hate being the loser in all of my brother's bets. Just once, I'd like to have the upper hand. And four hundred dollars.

"How could it not?" Juliet asks like we're talking about whether the microwave will cook popcorn. "Now to find the right guy." She looks around the university library, then pulls out her phone.

"What are you doing?"

"Looking at my contacts for eligible bachelors," She says, thumbing through.

"Does Michael know you still have all these numbers?" I laugh.

She freezes. "Hmm, I should probably delete them. But only after I find you the perfect guy." She resumes her scrolling.

Just what I want, one of her rejects.

"Or we could just take a walk around campus and ask the first hot guy we see," I say sarcastically, because this plan is a total bust. How am I supposed to find someone to be my fake fiancé for a night? Is there an app I can swipe right and connect with my perfect faker? There's an app for everything.

She looks up at me. "That's how you find creepers."

"Was that how you found my brother?"

A smile cracks her lips, and she puts her phone down. "Don't worry, I'll find you a non-creeper."

I nod my head. "Good, because if my fiancé ends up killing me, I'd be so bored haunting you for eternity."

She chucks a wadded-up piece of paper at me and I don't even try to dodge it.

"Wait," she sits up straight. "Jeremy is in my next class. He'd be perfect." She shoves her books into her bag and jumps up.

"Juliet. Wait!" But it's too late. She's gone. Well, she can find me a guy by herself.

"I heard you need a fiancé," says a deep voice to my left.

I jump and fall back in my chair. My knees hit the bottom of the desk and it knocks my pen to the floor.

An enormous man kneels to the ground beside me and picks up my pen. He holds it out to me.

"Want to fake marry me?"

He is the definition of a Tongan god. If that's even

a thing. But there's truly nothing else that could describe him. Dark features, chiseled jawline, and as big as an NFL lineman.

Air. Need air. My lungs aren't working. Because one, a random guy is fake proposing to me, and two, he is one of the most gorgeous men I've ever seen.

I've never been proposed to before, but I'm pretty sure the first rule is to not laugh.

Which is what I'm doing.

"What?" My giggle is juvenile, and this guy, whoever he is, will retract his offer any second now.

He stands and holds out his hand. "Sorry. I'm Noa. I overheard you and your friend talking and thought I'd offer my assistance."

Every word out of his mouth is rich and smooth. Can I marry him for real?

"W-why? Why would you want to do that?" I ask, plucking at the messy bun I'd mistakingly worn today.

"I need a date for my high school reunion."

I grimace then chuckle. "Ooh, a reunion? I'm not sure that's a fair trade."

"You see my dilemma." He shakes his head and sits down beside me.

I laugh again. Because I'm awkward and have no experience with men. "Well, when you put it that way."

"I'm no Thor, but I figure we can still help each other." He shrugs as if he makes business arrangements like this all the time. For all I know, he does.

"How do I know you aren't going to pretend to marry me then kill me to get my money?" I eye him.

His smile grows, and it's like watching the sunset; it just gets better. "Do you have any fake money worth inheriting?"

My face cracks and I laugh. "No."

"Then you're safe." He smiles, and I surprise myself by actually considering a fake engagement to him. This could totally work. He isn't just bigger than my brothers, he's a giant. A hot giant.

"But I should probably ask why you need a fiancé. I need to know someone won't steal a lock of my hair or something."

"Why would anyone do that?"

"Have you not seen these people?" He gestures to the average college students around us entranced by their books and laptops. "You never know who might want to steal your identity."

"I don't think anyone could pass for you."

He wiggles his thick brows. "Does that mean you find me attractive enough to consider me as a candidate?"

"Considering it." Halfway sold already. But I can't get Grant out of my head. What would he think if I showed up with Noa? Would he finally see me as more than his best friend's sister? It's a high hope, but it's all I have. If showing up with an attractive giant of a man won't make him see me, nothing will.

If nothing else, maybe Noa can help me move on.

"So why do you need a fiancé?"

I sigh and close my laptop. This story will take up the remainder of my study time. "I have three older brothers and they have been making bets about me forever."

His brows pinch together. "What kind of bets?"

"Let's see..." Where to even start? "They made a bet that I couldn't make the high school soccer team. So I did. Even though I hated it. They also made a bet that I'd never dare sneak out of the house after curfew. I did. And got grounded until prom."

"Sounds like they love you a lot." He says with a shake of his head.

I whirl back. "Did you not hear what I just said? They've been torturing me for years."

"Name one guy who hasn't tortured someone he loved in some way."

I open my mouth to say my dad, but he loves to scare my mom. Which she hates. But that's different.

"And then there's Grant. He's their best friend and even worse than them. He's always in the mix, making me angry."

Noa's eyebrows rise and he taps the table with a fist.

"What?" I ask.

"Nothing," he leans back. "So you want to prove to your brothers that you're more than just their entertainment?"

I bite my bottom lip. Is this completely insane? "I guess." The idea is still so new, but this feels like the only solution to my problems.

"Well then, should we do this? Should we enter a mutually beneficial fake relationship?"

Do I dare? My brothers have so little faith in me, and it's way past getting on my nerves. Noa is right. I want to be seen, and acknowledged by my brothers. And mostly by Grant.

"Let's do this." I hold out my hand. "I'm Lennox, by the way."

Chapter 5

Grant

I shouldn't be at work so early. Most people don't come in at 4 am. But I couldn't sleep.

My neighbors started a screaming match around midnight that ended with broken glass. I tried putting in my earbuds and going back to sleep, but I still woke up covered in sweat and shivering. All it took was one little thing to debilitate me back into the little boy I used to be, afraid every time my dad came home drunk.

Instead of grabbing my tools and getting ready to work, I head to the back room. It has the most space and is the coolest room in the shop. Plus, there is a pull-up bar above the door that Michael put there and forgot about. I grab my jump rope and retrieve the cinder blocks from outside the back door.

My own gym. Free and just as effective. I put in my earbuds and let the pounding music mask the world around me as I push through my reps. Sports had been my sanity in high school. I always pushed myself hard, and usually ended up playing alongside the kids a year older. Which was how I got to be good friends with Michael as well as Sean and Trent. My dad never came, which was for the best, seeing him would have just made me angry. But I was constantly angry, anyway.

At my mom for never giving us a chance, at my dad for choosing alcohol over me, and at myself for even caring. I didn't talk to my friends about my home life, and if they suspected anything was wrong, they were kind enough to not bring it up. I spent as much time as I could in their house; I was happier there than I had ever been in mine.

I drop to the floor and pound out as many push-ups as I can without slowing.

My grandfather was my saving grace. He taught me how to carve wood, and together we made a small box. On the lid, we'd hand-carved a lion, my grandfather's favorite symbol for bravery. Something I could only hope for. The bravest thing I've ever done was move out of my dad's house when I turned eighteen.

I haven't seen my dad since that night. He hasn't reached out to me either.

And that's ultimately what brings me to the shop in the middle of the night to do pull-ups until my arms shake.

I finish just before six. The guys will show up for work soon, so I need to hurry and clean up. Luckily, there's a shower in the employee bathroom.

I hurry inside and turn on the water. Mark Bentley has talked about getting rid of the shower to make a nicer bathroom, but he wouldn't consider it if he knew how often I have to come here to get warm water. I don't always get that luxury at my apartment.

I stand under the hot stream for longer than I planned and by the time I get out, it's six on the dot.

Crap. I'm going to be late to work even though I've been here for hours.

I wrap my towel around my waist and start digging through my bag for my shirt when the door opens.

I jump back, half hiding in the shower, but whoever

it is doesn't see me and continues into the bathroom.

And it's not just anyone. It's Lennox.

Is she reaching for her waistband?

I jump out from the shower and hold a hand out to stop her. "Wait!"

"Ahhh!" she screams, and it's like I'm watching her in slow motion. She turns back to the door but runs into it instead and bounces off the edge before I finally move to catch her.

She falls backward into my chest, and I wrap my arms around her to protect her fall. We crash to the ground in the small space between the sink and the shower. The tile is cold on my back, and I'm just as frozen. I think my towel is still intact, but I'm too terrified to check.

It's miserably silent, and then she speaks. "What just happened? Am I still asleep?"

I can't help it. "Do you often dream about half-naked men?"

"Grant!" She finally turns to look at me and whatever she planned to say next falls off her lips. Her eyes widen when they land on my chest, and my heart races.

"What is that?" She says, pointing at the tattoo on my pec.

I look down as if I have no clue what she's talking about.

"Where did it come from?" She asks again, her finger resting on the black ink on my chest.

I want to tell her what it means. But I can't. Not yet.

"Really, Lennox?" I smirk. "Have you never seen a man's chest before?"

Her cheeks go positively cherry and her lips part,

but no words escape.

If she asks again, maybe I'll tell her. Maybe I'll confess every feeling I've held in my heart for her if she would just ask.

"Lennox!"

I don't have time to move away before Trent and Michael burst into the small bathroom. Thank heavens Sean isn't with them.

Lennox scrambles away from me like she's been stung. I could try to pretend that the feeling is mutual, but all I want to do is pull her back to me. Where she belongs.

"What the heck is going on?" Trent looks ready to rip me apart.

I hold out my hand and slowly stand, securing the towel to my waist with my other hand. I don't need any more accidents here.

"Lennox walked in on me showering and fainted when she saw my abs." I'm smiling, but I'm pretty sure the beautiful girl beside me is not.

"Excuse me! You didn't lock the door! And I had to pee!"

"Lennox, men work here," Michael says with a scowl. "You always have to knock even if it's unlocked."

"She's right. I forgot to lock the door. That's my bad." I'd rather one of them punched me for supposedly taking advantage of their precious sister than blaming everything on her.

"Still Lenny, you should know this, you grew up in a house with three boys." Trent piles on the guilt.

A scowl covers her face, but it doesn't mar her beauty. "How could I forget?" She mutters before pushing past her two hulking brothers who just frown.

I'll go talk to her on my first break and apologize.

"Dude, when did you get so ripped?" Trent punches my arm.

"You punch like a baby," I say, but it doesn't stop me from rubbing my bicep.

"I need to workout with you," Michael says, self consciously rubbing his stomach. "I'm getting fat just by being engaged."

"I wasn't going to say anything," Trent says and immediately gets punched in the shoulder.

"Yeah, sure," I say to Michael, hoping to get out of this sooner. Some of us have jobs to get to or like clothes to put on. "Can I please change? Or would more Bentleys like to barge in?"

"Oh yeah. Sorry, bro." Trent walks out, but Michael doesn't follow him. He's wearing his rare, but intimidating big brother expression, and I'm squirming in this cheap towel.

"Are you sure there's nothing going on between you and my sister?" He folds his arms, pushing out his biceps. He's smaller than me though, so it's not the muscles that intimidate me, it's everything about this family. If I mess things up with Lennox, I'll be left with nothing. Again.

"Nah man, she just walked in, I told you." I ignore his intense gaze and pull on my shirt.

It's never taken me so long to get dressed.

"So there's nothing?" he asks again.

Gosh, I wish there was something. "Nope. She's like my sister."

He purses his lips and studies me like he's looking right through me. I'm about ready to yell, "Yes, I love your sister, okay. I have since junior year when she almost kissed that stupid Lucas."

He shakes his head. "That sucks. You're the only guy I know I can trust her with."

My jaw hits the floor.

"What?" It's out of my mouth without a second thought. I've watched him put every guy under a microscope and find all their flaws, and now he's rooting for me? This must be a trick. Another bet. Something.

He shrugs. "Too bad." He leaves, and I stand there dumbfounded.

There's a chance. He just gave me an opening. And I'd be an idiot not to take it.

I walk out the door, then turn right back around.

Pants. I need pants first.

Chapter 6

Lennox

Shirtless.

Grant was shirtless. And wet, and practically naked with only that towel on him.

And I made a complete fool of myself by crashing into him. But oh, what a wonderful moment that had been with his arms wrapped around me.

His body is like a cheese grater. All chiseled and muscled and one hundred percent capable of scraping my heart to shreds.

And that tattoo. I'm itching to open a blank canvas on my tablet and draw it. It was almost identical to the lion carving on the lid of the box he made me for graduation.

If lions weren't my favorite animals before, they are now.

I fan my face with the stack of plans my dad just dropped off. I still can't calm my racing heart. He caught me from crashing to the ground, and he held me, and all my lifelong dreams came true at that moment.

Until my brothers interrupted. They always crash in on my dreams, so I should have expected it.

Everything is always my fault or my lesson to learn. Why didn't Grant get chewed out for not locking the door? They treat him like a brother, but they treat me like an annoying little pest that they have to keep in line or play pranks on to get me to leave.

Which makes Juliet's idea and Noa's offer even more appealing. I can't wait to see my brother's faces when I show up at the party with my fake fiancé. Their heads will explode, and they'll finally see me as a woman. They'll have to. Or maybe I'll just marry Noa for real.

Okay, yes. I know how ridiculous that sounds. But I'm sure I could do a lot worse. That would require me to stop pining after Grant, though.

Which would be a lot easier if I hadn't just seen his bare chest.

"Hey, Len."

I jump and fall back in my chair, which, in this tiny office, is against the wall and my head doesn't stop until it hits it.

"Oh. Sorry." Grant says as he takes a few steps in.

He's fully dressed now. Dang it. I mean thank goodness.

I swallow. "Hi."

He gives me a smile, which acts as a warning to what comes next. He leans over my desk, letting that stupid cologne he wears drift all over me.

I take that back. It's not stupid. It's perfect and makes me lose my mind every time I'm near him. I want to spray it all over my room and never leave. Okay, I need to stop now before I make a fool of myself.

"I wanted to come check on you. I know you were pretty freaked out, seeing all this." He gestures to his torso, and my mind is right back in that bathroom.

Or is it the gutter?

I blink away from his broad chest and pull my brain back in the general direction of my body.

"What?"

"It's okay. The first time is always the hardest." He's not even bothering to hide his grin.

"That was not my first time seeing a man's chest!" But it was my first time seeing the tattoo on his chest. It must be new. I've seen him with his shirt off before when he's at our pool or working out with my brothers.

Is that drool on my lip? Yuck.

His eyebrows furrow. "Really? Who have you been cheating on me with?"

"Cheating?" I bark out a laugh that sounds very unladylike and then groan inwardly. "Sometimes I wonder if you even hear yourself when you speak." I turn my attention to my computer, which is off.

Crap.

As long as he doesn't come around my desk, he won't know.

"Are you sure you're okay? Or do you need to take a sick day after that heart attack?" He's still going strong, and I need to put a stop to this right now because it is way too close to the truth.

"Yeah, I had a heart attack," I admit. "Because the pudgy kid I knew in high school doesn't look so bad now."

He smiles because he knows I'm lying. He's never been pudgy, except maybe when he was a baby. I bet he was the cutest baby in the world.

"That's the closest to a compliment I'm ever going to get from you, isn't it?"

I grin. "Yep."

"You're cute. I'll take it."

My face burns and I pretend to do something very important on my computer. He has never called me cute before. How do I respond to that? "Sure. Yeah. Thanks."

Not like that.

"Okay." He raises his hands in surrender. "I'm done. I'm sorry."

His confident grin is replaced with a genuine smile. "I should have made sure the door was locked. And I'm sorry your brothers got mad at you."

I bite my bottom lip, trying to school my emotions over this sudden shift in the room. "It's nothing new."

"It still hurt you." He whispers, and I hate that tears sting the back of my eyes in response.

"I'm fine." Or at least I will be after I teach my brothers the lesson they deserve in exactly eleven days.

"You don't have to pretend around me," he says.

I swallow hard at the seriousness in his voice. If I didn't pretend around him, he'd know how much I cared about him and he'd never come near me again.

"Okay." I lie and turn back to my blank computer.

"Hey, Len?" His rough voice sends tingles through my veins.

I raise my eyes to him, slowly, carefully, like I'm looking at the sun. Because even though I know I shouldn't, I still do it. "Yeah?"

He leans in, his smile growing with each inch he closes between us. I resist the urge to lean toward him. It wouldn't take much to make our mouths touch. Just once, I want to kiss those tempting lips.

"Your computer isn't on yet."

That wasn't a line, but wow, it sure sounded sexy. My heart races as my sweat glands kick into overdrive.

"See you later. Try not to fall for anyone else while I'm gone, okay?"

"Ha. Never."

He grins and pats my desk before leaving, and I slowly die. Why did I just say that?

Chapter 7

Lennox

"Dad said the boys made another bet," Mom says as we prepare Sunday dinner.

I raise my eyebrows at her. "Does that surprise you?"

She lets out a heavy sigh, like she's tired of fighting this battle. "No. What is it this time?"

"I have to bring a date to the work Christmas party."

"Oh honey, no."

"It's just a work party," I grumble, mixing spinach into the salad. "How bad can it be?"

"How bad can it be?" My Grandma Bella laughs from across the table. "It's a party put on by your father."

She has a point there. Most people think my dad is super chill, but when it comes to Christmas, he tends to go overboard with the crazy train.

One year, instead of having a regular Santa, we had a sock puppet Santa. It was hard to sit on that one's lap. Another year, he started a new Christmas Eve tradition by buying me and my brothers paintball guns. I was eight. Pictures that year featured two black eyes and zero smiles.

"It will be fine," I assure both of them and dump the tomatoes into the tossed salad. "I already have a date."

I don't appreciate the way both of their eyebrows fly up. Is it really so hard to believe that I can get a date?

"You do?" Mom asks.

"How hot is he?" Grandma jumps in.

"A ten." I grin.

Grandma claps, and mom looks at me like she isn't sure I'm the same daughter she gave birth to. I debate telling my mom the *real* plan, but I can't while my grandma is present. That woman can't be trusted.

"When do I get to meet him?" Dad asks, wandering into the kitchen and stealing a piece of the pork my mom is shredding.

"Uh…" in all my grand ideas about getting my brothers back, I'd forgotten about this part. "You were serious about that? I thought you only meant it for Sean."

Dad's brows pull together in a hard line. "I guess you're right. But I'd still like to meet the boy my daughter is dating."

Oh, yikes. Dad is going to be pissed when I come with my pretend fiancé. "You know, Dad, I—"

"Did I hear right? Is little Lenny dating someone?" Michael asks as he walks into the room with Juliet on his arm, looking as innocent as she always is.

"He's just a friend," I say. The less he suspects, the better.

"Does this mean I'm going to be a hundred dollars poorer next week?"

"Yes, sirree." I grin, and to my surprise, he smiles too. Like he doesn't mind wasting money on me. Which has never been the case before.

My smile fades. "Why do you look so happy?"

"Why wouldn't I be happy? My little sister is dating again."

Now I know he's lying, but my other brothers and Grant walk into the kitchen, so I decide to drop it.

"Grant, did you hear that?" Michael says, and my face pales. "Little Lenny has a boyfriend."

That was *not* what I said.

Grant's dark eyes bore into my soul, and I want to know what they see.

"Cool." He says and he and Trent immediately go into the other room. To play pool, I assume.

The air whooshes from my lungs. *Cool?* Yesterday I saw him in a towel and now all he can say is cool? And hadn't he flirted with me a little? I've been out of the game for a while, but I'm pretty sure what he did in my office is called flirting.

Michael and Sean trail after them, and as soon as they're gone Juliet pulls me out back to the pool.

"So that guy, Noa, is he going to do it?" she asks.

I texted Juliet and told her everything after Noa left the library the other day.

"Yeah. He needs a date for an event as well, so I think it will work out." I rub my upper arms. It's only fifty-five degrees today which might as well be North Pole weather for my Arizona blood.

She nods and starts twirling a strand of hair. "I'm starting to second guess my grand plan. We know nothing about him. What if he's a total creep?"

I dismiss her concerns with a wave. "I stalked him on all the social media sites. He even gave me his mom's number. I didn't call her though."

"What if that's his play? He acts like the perfect gentleman and then bam! You're a five cow wife on an island with triplets on the way."

I blink. That sure escalated quickly. But it's good to see that she's moved on from her addiction to true crime. "First, I'm offended. Shouldn't I get at least ten cows? And second, think of the vacation. Until the babies are born, anyway." I've heard kids tend to ruin things.

"I'm serious, Len. I know I'm just your almost sister-in-law, but I love you and I couldn't live with myself if something bad happened to you because of me. Maybe you shouldn't do it. We can find another way to get back at your brothers."

I watch her hand furiously twisting her hair. Shortly after we first met, she told me she had anxiety, but until now, I had only associated that with her hair twirling. But now that I'm paying attention, I remember all the times she has doubted herself. Shopping with her is a nightmare. She can never decide and half the time she ends up taking things back, anyway. But she doesn't need to second guess this plan.

I grab her hand before she pulls out that chunk of hair. "There will be no cows or Tongan babies. I promise. But I'm doing this."

She takes to biting her lip instead. I'm not stopping that one. "Okay, just update me every five minutes when you're out with him, so I know you're safe."

I smile, trying to help her calm down. "I'm a big girl. I'll be fine. You can track my phone the whole night if you want. Deal?"

She nods, though I can tell she doesn't want to. "Okay."

"Okay." I pull her in for a quick hug and thank the blessed online dating site who set my dope of a brother up with this angel. I didn't realize how much I needed a sister in my life until she came along.

Dinner is a loud occasion at the Bentley home. It's not just my brothers, though. It's grandma too.

"And then I told that evil old witch I'd be visiting

her in hell."

"Alright, Mom. I think you've had enough eggnog." Dad says, but it hardly stops him, or anyone else, from laughing at grandma's stories from the assisted living community.

She is so sharp she could probably tell different stories for three straight hours without repeating one. Which she often does.

I hope when I'm her age, I'll be able to tell my grandkids how exciting I used to be. I will have to do something exciting first.

"Grant, dear, how's your dad doing?" My mom asks, and the room goes still. She asks him this once about every six months, to be polite I'm sure, but we all hate it.

"He's fine," Grant says. He's given the same response for the past six years.

"That's good," Mom says, completely not reading the room. "I keep meaning to invite him over. Maybe for Christmas dinner."

My blood turns to ice, and I look at Grant, who is staring holes into his plate. "Yeah, maybe."

He's been around our family long enough to know exactly what to say to get people off his back, but I still hate that he has to do that. I can see it on his face every time his family is mentioned. I can practically feel the deep void in his life known as his parents. He kept quiet all growing up, but he shared just enough for us to know his dad was an aggressive drunk. I know nothing about his mom except that she left when he was a baby.

Grant keeps his eyes on his plate for the rest of dinner, and my heart breaks more for him with each passing second. He should be at his own home, with his own family. But he'll always have a place in ours.

After dinner, Grant helps with the dishes, like he always does, and then he and my brothers go out back to sit around the pool like they always do. They're so predictable. Grant still looks upset, though. While the other guys are talking and laughing, he's barely nodding, and smiling politely.

"Hey, Juliet," I say, catching her before she goes out back to be with her weird fiancé. "Want to prank the guys?"

"Oh, my gosh, yes." She puts the drinks she's holding on the table, and I take her to what we call the "mess room". Because it will always be a mess. No one cares enough to go through it and clear all this junk out. We just shut the door on it and pretend it doesn't exist. Mom wishes it didn't, but the rest of us love it.

"Paintball guns?" I ask, moving to the corner of the room where the more dangerous stuff is.

"Uh, no." Juliet pulls me back to the baby prank section. "I want children someday."

I plug my ears, but it's too late. "Ew. I can't believe you'd do that to the world."

"Oh no." Juliet chews on her lip.

"What?" I ask.

"I just realized this crazy Bentley gene is going to transfer to my children."

I laugh. "If you can't beat 'em. Join 'em."

She studies me like I just told her their kids will come out with tails. They shouldn't, but one can never be too sure. "Okay, what about paint balloons?"

"That's so lame," I mutter. "The last time I was out there they covered me with slime, and then confetti."

"Okay, so… paint and confetti?"

I shake my head. "Oh Juliet, we have so much to

teach you if you're going to be living with Michael."

I let her have her pick because despite what I said earlier, I would make a great aunt to their beautiful babies. Tails or no tails. We fill up sixteen balloons because I know we won't get more than two seconds to pull off our prank. And then two confetti cannons.

"Hey, Grandma, want to help?" I ask on the way to the deck above the pool.

She stands, wavering somewhat, but heads for the door like a woman on a mission. "I get Sean. He keeps prank-calling me. That little sissy."

Dad joins too, and then we are in line. Mom is stationed across the pool "checking the flowers" and with one little thumbs-up, we let our balloons fly. My first one drops on Grant's head and the second one just beside his phone on the deck.

Four guys jump up in unison, each covered in green paint and turn their heads upward, just as we release the next round of balloons. Mine splatters at their feet this time, but Grant is gone.

Oh no. Time to retreat.

I turn to run, but he's already halfway up the deck stairs. I dart for the door inside, but he meets me there.

"Don't do it." I brandish the confetti cannon in front of me, daring him not to come any closer.

His steps are slow, but he doesn't stop. I know that hungry look in his eyes well. And every time I see it, I wish it involved something other than revenge. "Come on Len, give in and it will be easier."

"Never." I shoot the cannon at him and sprint inside. I only make it three steps before his arms close around my waist and I'm being hoisted in the air. I should scream and make him put me down, but he's holding me, touching me. And now my problems are more apparent than ever. I only do this for his attention, because this is the only way I can get it.

"Put me down," I say, half-heartedly, because I know how this ends. With me being thrown into the pool. "I hate water."

"I know you don't," he says, almost to the bottom of the stairs, now.

That's true. I love the water and I'm usually in the pool all summer, but I actually did my hair today.

"Don't do this." I try to grip his back, but there's no extra skin to grab because he's ripped and covered in paint and why is that so hot?

"Sorry, Len. You know the rules."

And then I'm in the water. I know the rules. I mess with Grant, he gets me back. And yes, I secretly love it, but I still come up spluttering.

"Gah!" I look up shivering to see Grant's glorious grin. What I wouldn't do to always keep that smile on his face.

Water hits me from every side as Grant and my brothers jump into the pool beside me, and soon the water has a greenish tint to it.

Grant comes up next to me, shaking out his short hair, and then looks at me.

"I don't know why you keep trying. You'll never win." Grant says.

Gosh, I've asked myself that same question so many times over the last eight years. How many balloons do I have to drop on his head to get him to see that I don't want to win anything but him?

"I will," I say, more to convince myself than him.

"Just not today." He says and scoops me up and

throws me over his shoulder into the water.

I come up and immediately attack him. Tugging on his torso and climbing up his back, but it's like trying to move a mountain. Impossible without dynamite.

"What are you trying to do here?" he chuckles as I cling to his arm.

"Drown you."

"Oh." He nods. "Well, why didn't you say so?" He spins and puts his hands on my waist, pulling me beneath the water with him.

When we were younger, we'd have contests to see who could hold their breath the longest and now we're doing it again. Except, he never held me around the waist like this. And he never looked at me like that when we were young.

The rest of the world is somewhere above the water, but they don't matter when Grant's hands are around me.

He seems to realize this at the same time I do and he shoots to the surface, losing our game. We *were* playing a game. Weren't we?

I come up for air, and his worried eyes meet mine for a second and then he says, "I forgot to run this morning. I'm going to go do that."

He's going to go for a run? Right now?

I watch him walk away, taking in his hunched back and tired steps. I want to follow him and ask him what's wrong, but I can't because my brothers start dunking me.

They always ruin everything.

Chapter 8
Grant

It took me exactly 3.8 miles of running last night to forget the feel of Lennox in my arms. Don't ask me how I know the exact distance. It took me a few years to figure out that nothing can erase the thrill of her except 3.8 miles of sprinting until my legs ache. And after finding out she's got a boyfriend, I needed those 3.8 miles.

But then she walks into work, and those feelings are right back where they always are.

Under my skin and dancing around my heart.

I shake my head, remembering the twenty-year-old boy who thought he'd finally be able to tell her how he felt. She turned eighteen and graduated on the same day. That was my chance.

I ate dinner with her family for her graduation celebration and then afterward I pulled her aside to give her my gift.

It was a little cedar chest, identical to the one my grandfather and I had finished before he died. The one and only good thing I had in my possession. I had told her about the chest when we were younger and she'd been intrigued by the story behind it, asking me all kinds of questions and wishing she had a family heirloom to cherish. She knew I was obsessed with it, but she didn't know I was obsessed with her. So I stayed late in the shop every day and made her one, hoping to show her that I had little to give, but she'd always be the one holding my heart.

I had just reached for the box I'd tucked in the hallway dresser when her friend Via showed up, ready to hit the road and celebrate.

Lennox left immediately. So I dropped the gift on her bed and scribbled out a little note to go inside. I never confessed my feelings, never told her what that chest meant to me. She thanked me the next day when she got home and gushed about it for the next month. Her love for it meant more than any praise I'd ever received.

Now she's twenty-one. And I still can't get over her.

I used to date, used to look for someone to be the missing puzzle piece in my life, but I just ended up comparing every girl to Lennox. So I stopped dating completely.

But she didn't.

After talking to Michael at work on Friday, I'd been ecstatic. My plan was to make slow and steady progress toward Lennox's heart. I couldn't shift her perception of me overnight, so I flirted with her in her office. Yesterday, I planned on flirting more, but she has a boyfriend? I can't even wrap my brain around that one. But how can I blame her? She deserves someone much better than me. I'm not giving up on her. I never will. But if she never sees me that way, and if she falls in love with someone else, I won't be able to stick around because it will kill me to watch the woman I love fall in love with someone else.

It's that thought that has me walking up to Sean.

"Hey, wanna go to the club tonight?"

Sean almost drops the drill gun in his hands. "You're joking?"

I knew he wouldn't believe me easily. I haven't

exactly been a "fun friend".

"No. I'm serious."

"Yes," Sean cheers. "Trent owes me twenty bucks."

***

I regret my decision the second I step into the dimly lit club. I can't come here without thinking of my dad coming home wasted and ranting. For this reason, I'll never drink. I refuse to touch the stuff that ruined my life and my friends respect that.

The club is decked out in holiday decor. There are a few Christmas trees, giant bows on chairs, and mistletoe placed about five feet apart.

That's bound to cause some problems.

"Dude… hotties at the bar." Sean hits me in the arm and I look.

They look nothing like Lennox.

Sure, they're pretty, but they've got so much makeup on, I'd never recognize them without it. Yes, I know this from experience. My last girlfriend wore so much makeup I walked right by her in the store one day when she wasn't all made up. When she stopped me, I still wasn't convinced it was her, and I might have asked her to prove it. She responded by throwing a carton of strawberries at me, and I had to pay for them.

But in my defense… Okay, I have none.

You live and you learn, I guess.

So no, I'm not interested in these women. I'm still hopelessly attracted to the woman with blonde hair and amber eyes, who has a dusting of freckles across her cheeks and nose and looks adorable when she wears her blue light glasses at work. My eyes drift across the crowded room and land on a table a couple of yards to the right.

A woman like that.
Wait, what?
I weave through the tables. "Lennox?" I touch the woman's shoulder and she turns.
Her eyes go wide, and she looks behind me before using me to hide.
"What are you doing?" I laugh.
"Hiding from my brothers. What do you think I'm doing?"
I turn to see them approaching the women at the bar. "Don't worry, they've already got a bet going. They'll be occupied for a while."
She relaxes a little, but still sinks further down in her chair.
"What are you doing here?" I ask her. She's not drinking anything. I don't think I've ever seen her drink and I'm sure she's not here for karaoke night.
Her eyes get even wider, if it's possible, and for the first time, I notice what she's wearing. It's her black dress. It's not so short that it's revealing, but it doesn't stop me from doing a triple take every time I see her in it.
"Just waiting for a friend." She says, and fiddles with her purse strap.
"You're waiting for a date?" Her boyfriend? I shouldn't sound so shocked by this. She's a beautiful woman and probably dates all the time. But that's not a road I allow my thoughts to take. Ever.
Her gaze narrows. "Is that so hard to believe?"
"No. I didn't mean it like that." Crap, how do I get out of this. "I just didn't think you'd ever meet a guy here."
I think she's going to get angrier, but her gaze softens. "You're right. This is not my scene."
I know what her scene is. At home, in pajamas,

cuddled up in the corner of the couch with a romance book in her hands. The television has to be on though, because she can't read when it's quiet. She grew up with brothers, after all.

My ideal scene is sitting right there next to her, holding her in my arms, and changing the television from her boring dramas to something with a purpose.

"So why are you here?"

"I'm waiting for a friend. He's my uh...friend."

"Yeah, that wasn't convincing." Why am I gripping the chair so hard?

"I'm..." She doesn't have time to finish, because a man who looks like an Easter Island head sits down at the table.

Now I'm really gripping the chair.

"Hey, Lennox." The head talks. Like that creepy museum show.

I swear I've had nothing to drink.

"Hey, Noa. This is my friend Grant." Lennox addresses the head.

Why did she just call me her friend? I don't even like her right now.

"'Sup, man?"

I feel my head nodding, but I have no clue how it happens. I'm also sitting down in the chair I tried to squeeze the life out of. *What's wrong with me?*

Noa turns his attention back to Lennox. "So you wanted to talk—"

"About psychology," Lennox interrupts. "Yeah, I had so many questions."

My eyebrows furrow. "I thought your major was graphic design."

She nods her head so fast I worry it might fly off.

"Yeah, yeah, it's the... psychology of uh graphic design."

That doesn't sound right, but then again, what do I know? I never went to college.

"Right, psychology of graphic design." Noa leans back in his seat and I worry it's going to snap beneath him. "I have so many questions, too. Why don't I get us drinks before we start?"

"Just a soda for me," Lennox says, and Noa nods.

The second he's out of earshot, which means one foot away because the person singing into the microphone right now is trying to burst everyone's eardrums, I turn to Lennox.

"You cannot stay here with that man."

She blinks up at me like I'm speaking Chinese. Maybe I am. This club is doing funny things to me.

"He's just my friend."

"A friend the size of a mountain," I mutter and look around. I don't need said mountain crushing me tonight.

"That's rude to say." Lennox scolds me.

"No, it's not. Do you have any idea how dangerous the world is? Do I even need to tell you how many people get drugged in places like this?"

"Who got drugged?" Noa says, returning to the table with what looks like two sodas.

But one can never be too sure. He places one in front of Lennox, but before she can grab it, I steal it and take a sip. If that guy wants to drug someone, he's stuck with me.

Both of them give me a strange look as I swallow half the cup. It's just Coke. I think.

"Ignore him," Lennox says to Noa. "He's like one of my brothers."

Something flicks to life in Noa's eyes, and I don't

like it. Not at all. "Right. Your brothers." He nods his understanding, and then they go back to staring at me like *I'm* the crazy one.

I finally hand Lennox the drink. If the mountain drugged it, I'll start feeling it soon, right? "Well don't let me keep you from discussing graphic…psychology," I say and then laugh because that's such a funny name.

Holy cow, he did poison the drink!

Noa looks between me and Lennox, then stands. "Actually, I was wondering if you want to dance, Lennox?" He holds out a hand and gives her what he probably thinks is a charming smile. But Lennox isn't like every other girl. She won't fall for—

"I'd love to." She grabs his hand, and he pulls her onto the dancefloor.

I fix my gaze on them, slow dancing and whispering like they have some grand secret. She can dance all she wants, but I'm not leaving her alone with him.

I will finish this Coke, though.

Chapter 9

Lennox

"So, he seems fun," Noa says as we sway to someone's terrible cover of one of Billie Eilish's songs.

I sigh. "He's not bad. He's just protective of me. Like all my brothers, I guess."

He shakes his head and spins me out. He has so much strength, I nearly hit the couple next to us.

"If he thought of you like a sister, he wouldn't be trying to kill me with his eyes."

My cheeks burn, and I look at the table. Grant is still there, and Noa is right. He's definitely using his eyes as weapons right now. But that's where the passion ends. Grant doesn't like me.

"He's had a hard life. We're the only family he has. Trust me, that's all he thinks when he sees me." I hear the inflection in my voice. And Noa does too.

"But you don't want him to, do you?"

I try to laugh it off, but something about Noa makes me crumble a little instead. "I've never told anyone this," I say. "But yes, I like him. A little too much."

Technically, that's not true. I told my friend Marie in high school. The next day, she threw herself at Grant, and that's when our friendship ended.

"So this bet really is about more than just proving something to your brothers then. You want to make him jealous?" Noa asks.

"No!" I shake my head. "I'm not trying to…" It's all a lie. "Yes," I say. I don't know how he gets me to admit things like this. He's like the human version of truth serum.

"Well, pretending to be engaged to me will definitely make him jealous," Noa says with a grin.

I want to agree that this will all work for the best, but I feel terrible inside. I hate lying. "Are you sure you're okay with that? I don't want to put too much on you."

He shrugs one of his massive shoulders. "To be honest, I'm kind of using you that way too. My ex-girlfriend will be at my reunion. We've only been broken up for a few months, and I really don't want to go alone."

I can't believe what I'm hearing. This big, handsome man was rejected? "Whoever she is, she's an idiot."

He shrugs. "I used to think she was perfect. Now, I'm not so sure."

I smile up at this man I now consider a friend. "There is a perfect woman out there for you. Even if it's not her." I assure him. Women would run a marathon in heels for this man.

Noa spins me out again as the music drops off.

Thank goodness.

"Enough sappy talk. Let's do karaoke." Noa says.

"Oh no. That's all you."

His jaw drops. "You don't like karaoke?"

"I've never done it before."

"Why not?"

"Remember, I'm the shy girl who does nothing exciting which is why my brothers have to bribe me to get a date."

"Hmm," he nods like he understands, "I think you're so much more than that girl." And then I'm being pulled toward the stage.

I try to pull back, but it's completely fruitless. "Noa. Wait, I can't do this."

He pauses to look back at me. "Do you want that Grant guy to notice you?"

I don't respond, but he already knows my answer.

"Then you have to take chances."

My resistance fades and he gets me to the side of the stage without me realizing it.

The crowd goes silent the second my feet hit the stage. But I'm not sure if it's the crowd or my brain. I actually love to sing. In the shower, alone in the car, things like that. But I have never, ever, sung in front of anyone. Not even my family.

My eyes seek out Grant. He looks stunned. And then I see my brothers next to the bar, still flirting with some women.

For all that is good, please don't let them notice me.

"We're singing *Dancing With a Stranger*," Noa whispers into my ear just as the song starts.

"Do you sing?" This feels like something I should've have known before now. Heck, I don't even know his favorite color. Things I should probably know about the man I plan to make my fake fiancé.

He looks at me and grins. "I guess we'll find out."

Then he opens his mouth and... He can sing. Like oh my gosh, he can sing. I'm so startled by his angelic voice that I come in late for my cue. But something amazing happens as soon as I hit it. I don't want to shut down and hide behind the nearest table. I want to go for it. I keep my eyes on Noa, and he stares right back at me, encouraging me with his warm smile

I finally have enough courage to look at the crowd by the time the chorus hits, but I don't see anyone besides Grant. Perfect, handsome Grant. His lips are parted and he's looking at me like he really sees me. Not just looking through me to see my brothers.

Noa sings the next line and then pulls me in to dance. The people below us cheer, and I laugh because I have never felt so alive in my life. I've never had so much fun doing something so terrifying. My heart pumps in time with the music and I sing louder, not even caring if I'm off key.

I'm singing. In front of a crowd. In front of Grant.

I can do anything!

The song ends, and Noa dips me. The audience claps, and we hurry off stage.

"Oh, my gosh. You have an amazing voice." I tell Noa as soon as we are free of the speakers.

"Me? Did you hear yourself?" He gives me a high five. "You killed that!"

The embarrassment that I thought would hit me on stage finally washes over me. "I've never sung in front of people before."

"Maybe you should start. We can start a band," he says with a smile.

I laugh because he's the most free-spirited person I've ever met. "Yeah. Right after we get married."

My phone buzzes, and I pull it out of my handbag.

Juliet: Are you still alive?

I forgot she's tracking my phone tonight and probably terrified to see me at a club.

Me: It was touch and go for a second there, but I'm still breathing.

Juliet: Don't even play with me.
Me: *kissy face*

"You sing?"

I jump and drop my phone on the floor. "Grant."

"Why didn't you tell me?"

I look around for Noa, but he's moving in the opposite direction, getting lost in the crowd.

"I haven't told anyone," I say as I bend over to retrieve my phone before it gets stepped on.

He sticks his hands in his pockets and his eyebrows scrunch together. "Why would you hide something you're so good at?"

That's a good question. "I—"

"Dude, Lennox, I can't believe you did that." Trent says, sliding an arm around my shoulders. "Sean, you have to get up there now."

Sean is right behind him and my only saving grace is that they didn't bring their female entourage.

"I thought you were going to puke." Sean says.

There it is. The reason I hide. The reason I don't let myself be who I want to be. Because the people who should support me no matter what, are the same people betting against me.

I look at Grant, and there's sympathy in his eyes, like he just came to the same conclusion.

"I get to pick your song, Sean," Trent says.

Sean shakes his head but concedes. "Anything but Ariana Grande. I can't go that high tonight."

A drink is thrust in front of me as Noa reappears. "Thought you might want a drink after all that singing."

Three heads turn slowly toward Noa. "Who are you?" Trent asks at the same time Sean says, "What are you giving our sister?"

Noa holds up his hands in surrender. "It's a Coke."

"Nice try, buddy," Trent says, and for the second time tonight, someone else is enjoying my drink.

One minute I'm branching out of my comfort zone, completely free, and the next, I'm back in the pit of Bentley's, all trudging over each other.

I'm out of here.

"I'll see you later Noa," I say before weaving toward the door. Nothing good ever happens when my brothers are around.

"Lennox. What are you doing?"

It's Grant. I know it is, but I don't have the energy to turn around.

"Going home," I say, maneuvering around a plastic snowman by the door.

"No. I mean, what are you doing with that guy?"

I freeze, then turn slowly. "What?"

He scrubs a hand over his face like he can't believe he has to have this talk with me. "Come on, you don't date guys like that."

"Excuse me? How do you know what kind of guys I date?"

His lips purse, because he's thinking about it. He actually has to think about it.

"Let me help you out. You're right. I don't usually date guys like that, because I don't date. At all. You and my brothers have made sure of that."

His mouth hangs open, but nothing comes out.

"I think it's time I start having fun too," I say, then turn on my heel. It's not too warm tonight, but I still blast the AC as soon as I get in my car. I need to cool down because all I want to do right now is go back there and rip Grant's stupidly perfect head off. Or make out with him.

JENESSA FAYETH

It's really hard to tell which direction I could go when we fight.

Chapter 10

Grant

She's going to start having fun? I dislike how that sentence runs on repeat in my head. I don't want Lennox to have fun.

Okay. That's a lie. I want everything for her. But I selfishly only want her to find it with me.

I'm such a fool. What did I think would happen? That she would never fall in love, never find someone perfect for her? Someone who pushes her to dream, and to sing like she did three nights ago?

I can still hear her voice as clear as it was that night. It's the music in my head the whole time I'm out installing a job. I also hear that guy's voice.

That guy. He's trouble.

I can smell it from a mile away, but Lennox has always seen the best in people. Which is why I thought for sure she'd dated plenty of guys, probably all losers of course, but she hasn't. When she said that I was part of the reason for that, I couldn't help but hope that meant she was just as strung up on me as I was on her. But I could see the miserable truth in her eyes. I have only ever been a pain in her side.

I place a board on the saw stop and I start the blade. The machine whirs as I slide the board across the table. My thumb hits the saw blade. I don't move. Don't react. I can't process what's happening fast enough.

The machine shuts off, and I jump back. There's blood slipping down my hand, but the wound isn't deep.

"Rick!" I holler.

He looks up from the toolbox on the work truck, sees my bloody hand, and goes down.

"Dang it, Rick." He's always so unreliable.

I wrap my hand up in my shirt and head to the truck for the first aid kit. I rummage through the picked-over bandages until I find what I need. I finally release the compress to assess the damage. I don't think I cut through anything major. It sure hurts, though.

Funny how the things I don't react to, the times I freeze up, are the ones that still carry the most pain in my life. Every time I didn't stand up to my dad. Every time I tried to tell Lennox how I felt, but I just couldn't do it.

Those are the mistakes that leave the biggest scars and the most regret.

And I've been living my whole life like that. Watching everything pass me by in slow motion, too afraid to reach out and stop the machine myself.

After work, I take the long way home, enjoying the kids playing out in their yards while parents set up Christmas decor.

I want that.

I want the cookie-cutter house, the two point five kids, the happy holidays. All of it. But I'm never going to get it in my current state.

I turn down my street and almost hit the back end of a white van.

"What the—" Dozens of cars litter the road and people crowd around a smoking building. My building.

I shut off my car, not even caring where I parked it, and sprint towards the apartment complex. I see Tom and his two grandkids on the sidewalk, then Marge and Brent. Where's Patricia?

I search the crowd frantically for my elderly neighbor, but I can't find her. I don't even think, I just run right into the burning building.

But I only make it two steps in before firefighters are pulling me out.

"You can't go in there. The whole building is coming down."

"But my neighbor, Pat, she's in there." I protest, pushing against the bulky men holding me back.

"We checked every room, it's empty."

I stop pushing and allow them to guide me back to the sidewalk. I'm numb watching my home for the last six years turn from orange flames to blackened ruins.

It wasn't empty.

Everything I owned was in there. The box I made with my grandpa. The few pictures, books, and "homey appliances" I had.

I'm empty.

I fall to the curb, watching the destruction. I'm helpless, with nothing to do but watch everything crumble.

"Oh, there you are, honey. I was so worried." Pat braces her hands on my shoulders and I look up to make sure she is alright.

"What happened?"

Pat coughs and if I didn't know her, I would request the paramedics check her out. But she's been a heavy smoker for years and coughs like this all the time.

"They think the toaster oven in the empty apartment was left plugged in." She says with another cough.

A toaster. I almost laugh because it's ridiculous. Who knew one toaster could do so much damage?

"It will be okay, honey." She pats my shoulder and toddles off, likely to check on someone else.

The fire is out, but the smoke sits heavy in the sky, the final remnant of destruction.

"Grant?" The voice is so soft, it's almost like I dreamed it.

"Lennox?" I look up, but she's staring at what's left of my apartment complex. "What are you doing here?"

"My dad wanted me to come check on you. He said you got hurt on the job. But..." Her voice trails off, and she drops to the curb beside me. "What happened here?"

All I want to do is pull her close, hold her until the pain of this day is nothing but a distant memory, but I focus on playing with the edge of the bandage around my thumb.

"A fire," I say simply.

She says nothing. Just sits beside me, watching the firefighters finish the job. Her presence is all I need.

"I'm so sorry, Grant." She whispers.

I nod. I know she is.

"You can stay at our house," she says and gently touches my arm.

"I know, thank you. I'll figure it out." I should accept her help. Her family has been nothing but kind to me. But right now I can't think about anything except what I lost.

Her touch melts me enough that I drop my head. "My grandpa's chest was in there." Everything else was replaceable. Books and clothes were just that.

Lennox lets out a small gasp. "Oh no, Grant."

Her tenderness breaks down my walls and pain hits me somewhere in my chest and spreads through my body.

I don't think, don't react. A saw is coming for me again, but I can't move.

Lennox pulls me into her and I fall against her like a child, hoping a mother's kiss can fix everything. But it can't. Nothing about this can be fixed. That was the one thing I had. The one thing I truly cared about.

"It will be okay," Lennox whispers as she rubs my back.

I was wrong. There are two things I care about.

I sniff and pull away from her. "I know," I say. I can't sit here anymore. I stand up and she gets to her feet as well.

"Where are you going to stay?" Lennox asks.

"I've got a place," I lie. I hate lying to her. I have no idea where I'm going tonight. To my aunt's house, maybe? In my car probably. I have enough money saved up from the years I've been working with the Bentleys, but I was hoping to use my savings for a down payment on a house. I can rent a hotel room for a few days, but it's not a realistic scenario long term. I need to find a new apartment.

"Are you going to be okay?" Lennox shifts from one foot to the other.

I know she's aching to fix all my problems. She's always been like that. She can't even watch the commercials on television about the kids in Africa without pulling her credit card out to donate each time.

I love her tender heart. But she can't fix everything.

I fake a smile for her like this hasn't been the third-worst day of my life, beat only by the night my father came home raging drunk and admitted he'd never wanted me, and the day my grandfather passed away. "I'll be okay."

"But…" she pauses. "You just lost everything."

I look into her liquid amber eyes. I lost everything I owned in that apartment, but there's one thing that I could never live without.

"Not everything."

Chapter 11

Lennox

It's been two days since I've really talked to Grant.

He's drifted in and out of work like a ghost of himself.

I know I wasn't supposed to be there to see him at his breaking point. But I've watched him long enough to know when he's breaking, even when he thinks he's hiding it.

"Do you want my red or yellow dress?" Juliet asks, holding up the two options.

I lean my head out of the bathroom in her apartment to get a better look. Tonight is Noa's class reunion, and because getting a fake fiancé was Juliet's idea, she's in charge of making me beautiful tonight.

"Red?"

Juliet nods. "Yeah, good choice. Yellow would wash you out."

"Thank you... Wait." I glare at her, but she just grins.

"I'm kidding. You would look gorgeous in anything. Let's finish your hair before you put this on."

She resumes curling my hair, and I find my thoughts drifting to Grant again. I've only seen him from a distance at work, but I know he's tired. It's understandable. He just lost his home. His possessions. The cedar chest he made with his grandpa. Losing such a physical reminder of his grandpa must have killed him.

I remember when I found the box he made for me for graduation. It took me by surprise because I knew how much he had loved woodworking with his grandpa. How much he loved his grandpa, period. I had hoped that his gift meant something special, that the only reason he made it for me was because he had feelings for me, and the note on the inside had given me hope.

"Congratulations. I hope you fill up this box with things that make you happy."

Below that, he had started another word, then scribbled out until there was nothing but a blob of black ink. I'd studied it for days, wondering what else he had wanted to say. I had thanked him and mentioned it every time I saw him for the next couple weeks, but he'd just shrug off my praise like it was nothing. Maybe it was because he wasn't used to praise, or maybe he had just made the chest to be nice, and it didn't mean anything. Regardless, I filled my box with things that made me happy. Most of them with some connection to Grant. Like the leather bracelet he'd worn throughout high school. He'd given it to me after he graduated and I carried on his tradition.

I sigh and turn back to the mirror. Memory lane is a dangerous place to get lost.

I still can't help but wonder who he's staying with that would cause him to be so exhausted?

"So is Grant staying with Michael?" *Well, just come right out and say it, Lennox.*

Juliet drops the strand of hair in her hand and looks at me in the mirror. "Why would he be staying with Michael?"

So that's a no. Where would he be then? Trent and

Sean don't have a lot of extra space at their place, and I'm sure if he was staying with them, they'd be talking about it. They talk about everything.

"There was a terrible fire at his apartment complex Monday."

"What? Why didn't he say anything?" she asks.

"Because it's Grant."

I bite my fingernail, an old habit that only comes out when I'm stressed.

Where could he have gone? His dad is in town, but even though I don't know him, I know he wouldn't go back there.

"Do you...." No, he wouldn't. Would he? "Do you think he's sleeping in his car?"

Juliet seems to mull it over. "I don't know. I'll text Michael." She says, pulling out her phone.

I grab it out of her hand. "No, Juliet. He'll be ticked if he knew I told people."

"But he's like family," Juliet protests. "Family doesn't let family sleep in their car. He can come crash on my couch. My roommates won't mind."

"Ooh, how hot is he?" Karli, Juliet's roommate, hollers from across the hall.

My blood boils. I barely know Karli, but I don't want her anywhere near Grant. I don't want anyone else near him but me.

"We have three guest rooms in the house. He knows he's welcome to stay there." I say, fiddling with my bracelet.

Juliet studies me in the mirror. Something is going on in her head, but I don't know what. "Yeah. Of course," she says finally. "Okay, you're done. Go get dressed."

"Thanks, Juliet," I say and stand up to change. "I'm

actually kind of glad you got me to do this. It's been forever since I've been on a date." I should be embarrassed by my lack of love life, but even though I've only known Juliet for a year, I feel like she was always meant to be my sister. I can confide in her, trust her.

She smiles. "You deserve this, sis. Don't forget that."

"I won't."

***

I don't deserve this torture.

Reunions are terrible. It only took me three minutes into Noa's reunion for me to decide that I will skip all of mine. Everyone is talking to Noa. Like everyone. He must have been Mr. Popularity. He's introduced me to everyone because he's nice like that, but after the introductions, they all turn their attention back to the star of the show, ignoring my existence.

I don't protest when Noa pulls me onto the dance floor.

"Sorry about that." He says with a smile as he spins me around under the fake snowflakes dangling from the ceiling.

"For what? Being Homecoming King, Prom King, and leading the football team to victory three years in a row?" I give him a cheeky grin and he actually blushes. "You were obviously very well-liked in high school. I'm surprised you don't have girls breaking down your door to be your date tonight." In fact, multiple girls had attempted to get between Noa and I, but Noa had kept me close enough they couldn't.

He shrugs a shoulder, brushing off my compliments. "Not everyone liked me." I hear the hurt in his voice. He must be referring to his prior girlfriend.

"You said your ex was going to be here. Have I met

her yet?"

He shakes his head. "Nah, I haven't seen her."

"It would be hard to see her through the hordes of people always crowding you," I say. But love was one of those things that made other people disappear. I didn't need to see Grant in a room to know if he was there. I could sense his presence by the electricity coasting over my skin the second he was near.

One song turns into two, and then five, and by the time we break, my feet are killing me and so are my cheeks.

A microphone screeches and I wince. A woman wearing a Santa hat and what looks like bright red plastic wrap steps up behind the mic. "Welcome back to school Tigers!" she hollers, with a rawr that no one returns.

"Oh boy. That's Chelsea. Our self-nominated class president," Noa informs me.

"Why does that not surprise me?" I'm holding in a laugh as she continues to rawr at the uninterested crowd.

She finally stops and smooths down her hair. "Isn't it so great to be back at school? I feel like I never left." She says with so much glee, I'm not sure she ever did.

"Ladies," she purrs into the microphone. "I caught a glimpse of Mr. Ferguson earlier. He's as hot as ever and newly divorced. I call dibs."

My eyes widen, and my mouth gapes. It's eerily quiet. "What is going on?"

"I wish I knew," Noa says, looking as uncomfortable as everyone else in the room.

Cling Wrap Chelsea looks like the kind of girl Sean would date.

I wonder if she's a belly dancer.

"So, in the spirit of the moment, I have impulsively decided to name a reunion king and queen."

Oh, this should be good.

"All in favor of me as your reunion queen, raise your hand." She raises both of her arms in the air and waits.

The room goes still. I almost raise my hand out of pity, but I don't know this poor woman.

"Fine." She pouts and flicks the pom-pom on her Santa hat. "Everyone in favor of Claire Hawkins?"

A roar rips through the audience so loud I jump into Noa.

"We should go," Noa says, grabbing my arm and tugging me toward the exit.

"Why? It just got good!" I say with a laugh. I'm enjoying this now.

"Everyone in favor of Noa Reid for reunion king?"

Noa freezes. I freeze too, but the uproar is enough to get my blood pumping again.

"Look at that. You're king again." I smile up at him, but he doesn't return it.

"Get on up here Noa," Cling Wrap Chelsea says. "Come get your queen."

"Noa?" I say. "What's wrong?"

He swallows. "That's my ex."

Chapter 12

Lennox

I'm pretty sure Noa is two seconds from passing out. After Cling Wrap Chelsea practically dragged him and his ex-girlfriend to the middle of the dance floor, she insisted they dance.

Who does that girl think she is? This isn't high school, and for all she knows, they could be married to other people.

Wait.

No. I can't do that. Noa never said he wanted to get back together with his ex, but what if he does?

His feet are barely skidding along the floor and he is looking anywhere but at the beautiful woman in his arms. He looks miserable.

He glances at me over Claire's shoulder. I wish I knew him better to know if raised eyebrows meant get lost or save me now. I'm going to go out on a limb and go with the second one because he keeps fixing his collar like it's choking him.

They've only been dancing for a minute, but neither of them has said a word to each other, and everyone is looking on and whispering.

Time to give them something more to whisper about.

I put one foot in front of the other until I'm less than a yard away from them.

Crap. I didn't figure out what to say.

Claire sees me first and eyes me like I'm a pesky little fly.

Words. I need words.

"Lennox," Noa says, sounding relieved. Gosh, I hope he's relieved.

He drops his arms and strides over to me. "I missed my beautiful fiancé."

"Excuse me?" Claire screeches and it's like a mic drop in the room. All eyes are on us. "We just broke up four months ago."

Noa reaches for my hand and I let him take it. "It doesn't take long to find true love."

Her eyes narrow to little slits. "Is that some sort of jab at me?"

Noa lets out a heavy sigh. "No, Claire. It's not."

I squeeze his hand harder, reassuring him he's doing the right thing. I'm not sure what he ever saw in her, but she likely doesn't deserve him.

"Then this is a joke, right?" Claire shakes her hands in the air. "I said we'd take six months apart, then we'd get back together. You can't trick me into coming back to you sooner. I won't fall for it."

Can I slap her? I want to slap her.

I take a step forward, ready to fight this she-beast for mistreating my friend, but Noa pulls me back.

"You can keep the six months, Claire. I don't need them anymore." Noa says and without a word, pulls me to the door.

I wait until we are out the door before speaking up. "Isn't she going to be ticked when she finds out we aren't really engaged?"

"Yep." He says simply.

"I guess we will have to get married for real now." I try to lighten the mood.

Noa stops walking. "I dated her for seven years. Four months ago, I told her I wanted to get married. But she said she wasn't sure. That she needed six months apart to determine her feelings. Who dates someone for seven years if they aren't sure about their feelings?"

"Someone who doesn't know how good she's got it," I whisper. "Noa, I know it hurts, and I don't mean to be rude because I know you probably still have feelings for your ex, but I don't think she's as perfect as you once thought."

He scrubs a hand over his face and starts walking again. "Yeah, I was too in love with her to see it sooner, but you're right, she's not the girl for me. Thank you for rescuing me." He gives me an impish smile.

"You're rescuing me too." I shrug, and my heart breaks for the man who's been mistreated. He doesn't know what he's worth because of his awful girlfriend.

"Do you want to marry that Grant guy?"

I choke on the air in my lungs. "What?"

"Well, you obviously love him. Do you want to marry him?"

Gosh, why does that question hurt so badly? Probably because I spent my teen years dreaming of exactly that.

"What I want and what he wants are two different things," I say, dropping my gaze to pick at my red nail polish.

"We'll change his mind," Noa says.

Suddenly, I'm second-guessing this whole arrangement. "But is that the kind of guy I want? Someone who doesn't act until it's too late? Do I really have to make him jealous to get his attention?" Because what if this works, and I get his attention because he was jealous, but when the game is over, he no longer cares?

I can live a life without ever knowing what it's like to be with Grant. I've been living it for years. But I can't live a life with Grant and then lose him.

"I don't know," Noa answers.

I shake my head. "Alright, this is way too deep of a conversation to have without sugar."

"Agreed." He nods. "Wanna go grab a milkshake?"

"Yes. Absolutely yes."

He grins over at me. "Maybe I should have proposed with a milkshake."

"Eh. It would have been overkill."

"Because a fake proposal isn't overkill enough," he says and lets me into his Range Rover.

I laugh and buckle up while he gets in the driver's seat.

"You know, this is kind of weird though, isn't it?" He asks as he starts the car. "A girl flirted with me in the library the other day, and I told her I was engaged."

"You didn't!"

His cheeks turn red, and he scratches the back of his neck. "I did. And then I forgot your name, so I looked like a complete jerk. And now I'm going to have to hide from her until graduation."

"Good thing you only have one more semester," I say.

He bumps his fist against the steering wheel. "How about pizza? I need to carb load."

"For what?" I chuckle.

He gives me a serious smile. "Finals."

I throw my head back with a laugh. "Does that

work?"

"Yes. Carb loading is the only way to prepare for important events."

I doubt it's the answer to all of my problems. But... "I could go for some pizza."

Chapter 13

Grant

I've never been more humiliated in my life than when I showed up at my boss's house earlier this evening carrying two grocery sacks of toiletries and clothes. My only current belongings.

I spent two days convincing myself I didn't need anyone's help or pity. Then I remembered my commitment to myself and to my grandpa, to be brave. And sometimes, the bravest thing someone can do is admit they need help and then accept it when offered.

It took two days in a crappy motel to realize that the fire was a blessing. I hated that forsaken old building. I hated being lonely. And now, for a moment at least, I'm not.

I'm laying in a comfy bed, in a house full of luxury, and waiting for Lennox to get home.

Home. I like the sound of that.

I'd like it better if she wasn't on a date with that mountain man. Where did she even meet him? How long has she been dating him?

I realized something else while I was on my way over. If I'm here, I can keep tabs on this relationship. Then casually jump in with my unsolicited advice and not-so-subtle flirting. I should have come to my senses two days ago when she offered her help. Maybe then I could have convinced her not to go out with him.

How long is she going to be out with him, anyway? Is she kissing him?

I push myself out of bed. I can't torment myself like this all night.

The Bentley's go to bed at 10:00 every night. They have ever since I was a kid. Because at exactly 10:15, we would sneak out of the house and go cause chaos around town.

It's ten now, so I know they won't be awake. I take my time walking around the large family room and sitting room, admiring all the Christmas decorations and family photos where everyone isn't just smiling, they are truly happy. I can see it in their eyes, feel it in their smiles. I will do whatever it takes to put smiles like that on my family someday.

I move on to the next one of just Lennox. Her senior photo. It's one of my favorites because just looking at her, I can see in her eyes her excitement for the future.

I want to share that future with her.

I plop down on her favorite corner of the couch and text Michael. I'm going to get crap for this, but I need to know what he meant.

Grant: Why did you say I was the only guy you could trust Lennox with?

His response is immediate.

Michael: Because I know you'd never try to take advantage of her.

Such a big brother answer.

Michael: Also, because I could whip your butt. It's such a hassle trying to maintain dominance.

I throw my head back with a laugh and text him back.

Grant: Maybe if you spent as much time working

out as you do making out with your fiancé, you wouldn't have to try so hard.

Michael: I take it all back. Stay away from my sister forever.

Grant: Are you using reverse psychology on me?

Michael: Is it working?

Yes.

I smile and put my phone back into my pocket. I'm not ready to admit to anyone besides Lennox my feelings for her. But for the first time, it's not Lennox's family's approval I'm worried about. I'm worried about hers.

I turn off the light and head back down the hall to my room. I know this house like it's my own. Which is the only reason I scream when I turn the corner, only to hit something that's not supposed to be there.

"Ahhh!"

I jump back and flip on the light. "Gosh, Lennox you scared me."

She looks at me in disbelief. "I scared you? What are you doing in my house in the middle of the night? And why do you have such a girly scream?"

I ignore her last question. "Middle of the night? It's a little after ten. How old are you?"

She lets out a sigh. "Not old enough for high school reunions."

I quirk an eyebrow, but she doesn't elaborate.

"Wait." She looks up at me, and I fall captive into those big amber eyes. "Are you staying here? Did the great Grant finally accept someone's help?" She asks in disbelief.

I scratch the back of my neck. "I'm sorry I turned you down at first. I just…didn't want to be anyone's pity project."

She pulls a bobby pin out of her hair and a long blonde curl falls in front of her face. "Accepting help is different from being pitied."

I know this. I do. But I'm still working on accepting it.

"Well, I'm here now, your wish came true." I smile when her cheeks turn pink. "Do we start with a movie night? Or a manicure?"

She smiles, then yawns. One yawn turns into two, then three, and I'm afraid she's going to fall right over in the hall. "I'm too tired. How about a slumber party?"

My heart ramps up and I can't help the smirk from overtaking my lips.

"Oh, my gosh. I did not just say that." Her face goes as red as her dress and she turns her back to me.

I could tease her endlessly for her slip, but her brothers do that already. And I don't want to be like her brothers anymore.

"Let's save the manicure for tomorrow," I say, then change the subject. "How was your… date?" Ugh. That's such an awful word.

She looks at me and lifts an eyebrow. "It was fine. Wait, how did you know I was on a date?"

I turn and walk back to the kitchen, my throat suddenly dry. "Your mom mentioned it."

"Ah," she says from behind me.

I take a sip of water then turn around just as she shrugs out of her jacket.

My mouth runs dry when I see what she's wearing. It's too red and too gorgeous and much too tempting.

I down the whole glass.

"You wore that?" I ask.

Did my voice just squeak?

She looks at me like I just said my name is really George Washington. "Yes. Why?"

"It's a dress." A very beautiful dress on an even more beautiful woman. How on earth was she allowed to leave the house like that?

She crosses her arms. "Thanks for noticing. You know my date told me I looked pretty."

"You do." I try to fix the damage I've done by being a territorial caveman. "Look pretty."

Her cheeks turn ever so slightly pink and she looks away. "Thank you."

She looks gorgeous. I want to tell her how gorgeous she looks even when she wears that unicorn onesie thing she got for Christmas last year. But there's a problem in the way of me confessing my feelings for her. A big, mountain-sized problem. I'm not about to stop Lennox from being happy, even if it means she doesn't end up with me.

"So you're dating that Noa guy?" I ask.

She turns back to me, her eyes widen, and she starts picking at her thumbnail. "Yes."

No, that's so much worse than I thought. "Why?"

She narrows her eyes at me. "Because that's usually what people do when they like someone. They date them."

Her words suck the air from my lungs. She likes him? It's happening. I'm losing her.

My throat hurts and the room spins.

"Not always." I shake my head.

Her brows furrow. "What?"

"Sometimes when you care about someone, you stay away. Even if it's the last thing you want to do."

Her lips part, but I turn and walk away before she

can speak. Because I can't explain that one to her. Not when the woman I love is falling for someone else.

***

Lennox hasn't been around for the last two days. She's been off taking finals, and while I'm glad I don't have to explain what I meant the other night, it's not helping me win her over.

Every time she's gone, I picture her snuggled up with Noa. And then I want to gag.

It's just my luck that the second I get the green light from Michael, I find out she's dating someone else.

I told myself I wouldn't interfere in her relationship, but when I'm around her, I can't stop myself from wanting to get closer, pester her, and flirt with her. I'm a grade schoolboy with a crush on a girl but all I can do is pull her pigtails. And if she happens to fall for me instead of the big kid on the playground, who am I to judge?

When I get back from work, I go for a run and then use the Bentleys WiFi to look for an apartment.

I've been looking every day, but the rental market is crazy right now, and I hate every available option.

I lean back on my bed frame. I'm sick of wasting my money on a crappy apartment. I don't want to go home to an empty apartment anymore. I want a house. A home. And a hope that I'll find someone to share it with me. I want a yard where I play soccer with my kids and a kitchen where I turn on soft music and dance with my wife after dinner.

For the fun of it, I change my search setting from renting to buying. I add four bedrooms, three bathrooms, and a half acre lot size.

I click submit. The first five are way out of my price

range. But the next one... there's a big open living space, with two double doors onto the back patio. The cabinets are dated, and the rooms need some touching up, but I can do that.

I sit up straighter and click through all the information in the listing. It's only twenty minutes from the shop. And ten minutes from the Bentleys.

This is it. This is my house.

I can already see Lennox sitting on the couch reading her book, and me serving her breakfast in the morning at the little bar.

I want this.

The price is still more than I have in my savings account, which means I won't be able to pay for it outright, but the loan for the rest of it will be doable.

I jump off the bed and haul my computer down to the house office. Mr. Bentley knows a lot about real estate. He'll know if this house is a good deal, and talk me out of it if it's not.

But he's not there.

"Oh, Grant!" Ms. Bentley says as I walk past the living room. "I need help pulling the tree out of the attic. Mark promised me he'd get it out last week, but as you can see, that hasn't happened."

I set my laptop on an end table. "Of course. I'll go get it," I tell her, already heading up the stairs. It's the least I can do while staying here rent-free.

Ms. Bentley is a pro at decorating. She's already decorated the rest of the house in red and gold, but their giant tree is still missing from the family room.

I locate the tree in the back of the attic and weave through the boxes to get to it. Getting it out of the attic isn't the hard part. Getting it down the stairs is. The tree and I get wedged in the middle where the stairs turn and it's not budging.

"Hey, Ms. B!" I holler. "The tree is stuck. How does Mark get it down?"

"Oh no." Ms. B comes running up the stairs. "I don't know how he does it. Did you try getting behind it to push?"

I eye the small gap the tree is offering. "I don't think I can get through there."

"Shoot. Let me see if Lennox is here. I bet she'd fit."

"Oh. No. I can totally get it. Don't bother her." I hurry to persuade Ms. B that I'm fine. I'm a man. I can move a fake tree. But the tree isn't being so cooperative. It's as stubborn as it is stuck.

"Hey. My mom said you need help."

Lennox.

I sigh and accept defeat. "The tree is stuck."

"Ah." She nods and flexes her biceps. "You need the big muscles."

A grin creeps onto my face. "Wow, weapons like that should come with a warning label."

She flexes again. "I could destroy you with my pinky."

My grin fades. She could destroy me with even less than that.

"Alright." She hikes up her pants and pats her biceps. "Let's see what we're working with here." She looks all around the staircase, folding her arms while rubbing her chin.

"What are you doing?" I laugh.

"Being a man. I thought it was obvious." She looks at me with a hint of challenge in her eyes.

"Because all men hike up their pants before getting

to work?" I ask, amused.

"Clearly." She makes a show of pulling her pants up again. "I think my dad usually brings it down in pieces."

It comes apart? That would have been nice to know.

Hmm. I move cabinets for a living. I'm paid to get things from point A to point B safely. But a synthetic tree stumped me. "Yeah, that would have been much smarter."

"I'll give you a pass this once." She winks then gets on her hands and knees. "I'll crawl through that hole and push from the other end. Get ready to catch it when it goes flying."

"Will do, muscles." I laugh and very purposely do not watch her crawl up the stairs.

"Um," she says a moment later.

"What?"

"I'm stuck."

I lean over and...shoot back upright. There's absolutely nothing to see there. "Can you back out?" I ask, a slight waver in my voice.

"Uh," I hear her moving around. "No. There's a branch sticking in my rib."

"Okay." This isn't good. "Try twisting maybe?"

She moves enough to make the tree branches move, but she's still stuck.

"I hate to say this, but I need some help." She sounds as reluctant to ask as I am to offer in her current predicament. But I can't just leave her stuck there.

"Okay, um, I'll try pulling you out." I bend down behind her. Then freeze. Where do I put my hands?

"Are you going to do anything?"

"Uh. Yeah." I can touch her. I've done it countless times before. I'll have to run later, but it's a sacrifice I'm willing to make.

I slide up as close as I can get and wrap my hands around her slender hips. I pull.

"Ow," she grunts.

I drop my hands. "I'm sorry."

"No, it's fine. Just pull a little harder. I'm getting claustrophobic."

"Are you sure?" I ask. I don't want to hurt her. It's the last thing I ever want to do.

"Yes!" she yells.

I don't need to be told again. I grab her waist again and yank. All at once, I lose my hold of her, and my balance on the stairs, and I roll down the stairs.

My head hits the wall, then the stair, and the wall again before I come to a stop on the tile. I catch my breath just as Lennox falls on top of me.

"Ow," she says and I hold in a similar groan.

I can't move. My back and head hurt, but it's more than that. I don't *want* to move. I'll take a tumble down the stairs any day for a moment like this.

"Are you okay?" she asks and rolls to the side.

"I will be." I breathe. "In a minute."

I don't have a minute, though. Because the next thing I know, the Christmas tree is barreling into us.

Lennox rolls into my side, using me as a shield. Branches scrape up my arms and face.

When it comes to a stop, I don't want to breathe. Lennox's hand is on my chest and I don't care that a fake Christmas tree has gotten the best of me three times now.

Lennox's head pops up. "I'm sorry. I think you got the worst of it," she says, tracing a finger along my cheekbone. There's no sting though, just pure fire.

Her lips are so close. I wonder if they feel as soft as they look.

Footsteps pound into the hallway, followed by a gasp. "Oh my! What happened?"

Lennox and I untangle limbs and branches and slide out from under the devil tree. On second thought, the family room looks better without it.

I offer Ms. B a half-smile. "We got your tree."

Chapter 14

Lennox

Mom is in the middle of making Sunday dinner. I usually help, but I can barely move today. I'm still finding new bruises from falling down the stairs yesterday.

I open the freezer and pull out an ice pack. I shut it, then jump when I see the twins standing there.

"Heard you and Grant got your butts kicked by a Christmas tree," Sean says and tries to put a Santa hat on me.

I swat it out of his hand, and it falls to the ground. Why does mom still invite them over for family dinner?

"I heard they were wrestling, and the tree wanted to join in," Trent says, and they both laugh.

I don't. I haven't heard the end of this since it happened yesterday. Everyone's versions are different, but mom's telling of the story is always the same. People hear what they want to hear.

I slam my ice pack on the counter and my brothers jump. "What do you want from me?"

The twins look at me, then at each other. "I think she's on her period," Sean attempts to whisper.

All I see is red.

"You would know, right, Sean?" Grant steps up beside me, and just like that, my anger fades away.

I look at him and at my brothers, who seem just as surprised as I do. My heart is beating a million miles an hour. So this is what it feels like to have someone stick up for me.

"Let's see who's crying like a girl when I kick your butt." Sean retorts.

Grant sends me a wink, then smirks at Sean. "Think you can take me down or do you want to go ask the tree for advice?"

Sean stands up straighter, and it's almost comical when he pushes his chest out. "Let's find out who's the real man." He leads the way to the back patio.

Grant shoots me a smile then trails after him.

I find myself following them to the door, but instead of continuing to the grass with them, I stay inside the back door. The stupidity of their "real men" competitions never ceases to amaze me. I don't know how many times one of them has ended up with a bloody nose or worse. But somehow they always come up laughing and smiling.

I don't understand men.

"Hey," Juliet says right behind me. "What just happened?"

I shake my head because I don't even know.

I watch Sean shake out his arms, while Grant just stands there smiling.

"I'm an only child, so I can't completely relate to what those guys put you through, but I know, deep down, they really do love you. They just have a weird way of showing it."

I blink and turn to face her. "Sorry. Say that again. I think I just hallucinated."

She nudges my arm and starts playing with her hair. "I think sometimes brothers just need a kick in the pants to realize that their baby sister isn't a baby anymore. Which is why you're doing this thing with Noa."

"Yeah." I nod and sigh. "I just wish I didn't have to pretend to be engaged to make them see me."

"They're just slow learners." She smiles. "Now, are you and Noa all set up for Saturday?"

I turn back to the show outside. Sean is trying to get the first move on Grant, but Grant keeps skirting his grabs. "Um? I guess."

"Well, are you or aren't you? Your brothers won't believe it unless you sell it. You got to make them believe you're in love."

"How am I supposed to do that?" I ask half-heartedly.

Juliet looks at me and releases her hair. "Well, have you ever been in love before?"

Yikes. There it is. The question I've been hiding from for almost a decade. "No. Nope."

Juliet purses her lips like she can tell I'm lying. "Really? I always thought you had a thing for Grant?"

"Grant?" I yell, then jump away from the window. "Ha!" I laugh, and it's super loud and childish. "No way."

Sometimes, when you care about someone, you stay away.

Grant's voice keeps ringing through my head. At that moment, the air between us had been charged with tension and anticipation, and for an instant, I thought maybe he was referring to me. But why would you stay away from someone you cared about? Maybe he was talking about his parents. Though, I can't help but feel like that's not what he meant.

Juliet's eyebrows furrow. "Really? I always assumed there was a little something there."

I look away and swallow. "You know what they say about assuming."

"Huh. Guess I was off base. Anyway, just pretend Noa is your dream guy and you never want to let him go." Juliet says like its oh so easy to pretend to be in love.

Is that how I act about Grant? All I think about when I'm with him is wanting to kiss him. But I don't do that with Noa. This already feels impossible.

"What if Noa tries to kiss me, to really sell it?" I ask her, my breath coming faster just thinking about it. How can I think about kissing Grant without having a mini panic attack? Maybe because I know it will never happen, so I have nothing to fear.

She scrunches her eyebrows. "Would you want him to?"

"No!"

"Then it's fine. Just tell him to kiss you on the cheek if necessary, that should be enough."

I'm not convinced, but I nod my head.

She puts a hand over mine. "You don't have to do this if you don't want to."

I think back over every prank my brothers have played on me, every time they've gambled with my life, and my worries fade away. They deserve this.

I shake my head and smile. "I'm doing this. Let's see if they can take it as good as they give it."

They better. I really don't want to be thrown in the pool again this year. It's getting too cold.

***

"Sean, when are you bringing your date over so I can meet her before the party?" My dad asks after we've all finished dinner.

Sean is mid-bite of cake and freezes. "You were serious about that?" Little chocolate crumbs tumble from his mouth, and I gag. I catch a whiff of the fresh cinnamon my mom keeps in the house during the holidays and my stomach settles.

"Of course, I was serious. Why wouldn't I be?" Dad asks.

Sean swallows and looks around the table. "Um, I guess I can text her." He fires off a text and the rest of the table grins. Sean has a knack for dating eccentric girls. Mixed with his own spirited personality, it's always too much. We never miss a chance to meet one of his dates.

Twenty minutes later, while we are all watching football, the doorbell rings.

Sean looks nervously around the room, then goes to answer it.

"Alright guys, be cool," Dad warns us.

I meet Grant's eyes and know that's not his plan. So it's not mine either.

Sean reenters the family room with a girl, who looks normal at first glance, but looks can be deceiving.

"Hey guys, this is Rachel." Sean introduces her, and then he goes around the room introducing each of us. After he finishes, it's her turn to speak, and I'm so excited I can't even wait.

"Hi y'all. I'm so happy to meet ya." She's got a southern drawl that sounds fake.

Strike one.

"I actually brought my best friend here as well."

I look behind her, assuming another girl came in with her. Maybe Trent's date, but instead, she opens her bag. I'm guessing it's a dog. Which is fine. I like dogs as much as any other person. I wouldn't bring my dog the first time I met someone's family, but—

"It's a snake!" I don't know if it's me who says it or someone else, but we all jump. Dad is across the room in a flash, and Juliet hides behind Michael.

Bentleys aren't afraid of anything. Except snakes. But it's not an irrational fear. Dad used to work at a pet shop as a teenager that had a few. One day, he was holding a California King Snake out to show a customer, and it wrapped itself around his neck. The shop owner rushed out and saved him, but Dad quit on the spot. Now, every time Dad tells the story, the snake gets bigger and deadlier. Last time he said it was a giant boa constrictor. Needless to say, we all steer clear of the forbidden species.

"Oh, Noodles is just a little thing. He won't hurt y'all," Rachel says, trying to calm everyone down.

It doesn't work. One, because she's lying. It's not as big as dad's "boa constrictor", but it's not a little water snake either. And two, I'm never eating noodles again.

"Rachel. You never said you had a snake." Sean backs away from her.

Now I'm closer to her than he is. Nope. That's not a game I'm playing. I back up into Grant, who knows we're all crazy but keeps coming back for more, and he puts himself between me and the snake.

"Are you okay?" he whispers.

"Yes. Unless she lets that thing free in here."

"Sean." Rachel turns a pout on my brother. "I thought you said you liked pets."

Sean jumps back as Rachel steps closer. "I-I do like pets. But snakes are not pets. Dogs are pets. Maybe even hamsters. Not reptiles."

She hugs the snake to her chest and a tear slips down her cheek. "That's just cold-hearted."

"I think reptiles are cold-blooded," Trent says. "They'll get along. They just need some time to warm up to each other."

I can't stop myself from laughing, but I don't want to be rude to Rachel, so I bury my face in Grant's back. His shoulders shake, and I know he's trying really hard not to lose it.

"I can't believe you would make out with me and then treat me like this." Rachel puts the snake back in her purse and stomps toward Sean, who, like an idiot, runs away.

His face is red, which is a rare occurrence for him.

"This is gold." Michael pulls out his phone, but Juliet slaps it out of his hand.

"I didn't know you had a pet snake!" Sean is on one side of the kitchen island now, and Rachel on the other.

"Yeah, well, I didn't know you *were* a snake!" she yells. "I'm so sorry Noodles, I didn't mean…" She looks at her purse, then opens it wide. "Noodles?"

It's at this point that all hell breaks loose. Everyone runs to the center of the family room. My dad may or may not be screaming. I'm a good daughter, so I won't tell anyone, but he's totally screaming.

I jump onto the couch, and Grant hops up beside me.

"Sean, help me catch him," Rachel says, frantically grabbing at the snake slithering around the table and chairs.

You'd think if you kept a snake as a pet, you'd know how to catch it.

"Yeah, you'd think, wouldn't you?" Grant says.

Oops, I said that out loud.

"How do you want me to catch it?" Sean jumps

when the snake slides over his foot.

"With your hands, idiot," Rachel growls.

"I'm going to pop some popcorn, does anyone want some?" Trent asks.

"Trent!" My mother scolds and hits his shoulder.

"I can't believe I let you take my first kiss." Rachel is sobbing now.

Sean freezes. "That was your first?" He looks absolutely horrified, and I almost feel bad for him.

But not bad enough to butt in. He totally had this coming.

"Wow, this just gets better and better." Grant laughs beside me.

I hope I don't regret my first kiss. I inhale, and Grant's cologne momentarily paralyzes me. If my first kiss is with him, I won't regret anything.

"I never want to see you again," Rachel cries. I must have zoned out because now she has the snake back in her bag, at least I hope so, and is walking toward the door.

"You and me both," Sean grunts.

"Sean Bentley, you walk that woman to her car right now." My mom reprimands him, and he scampers off.

The minute he's out of the room, everyone laughs.

"Good thing we got that out of the way tonight." My dad sighs and wipes his forehead.

"I don't know. I would have paid to see that at the party," Grant whispers to me. His breath tickles my neck and it does all kinds of ridiculous things to my insides.

"He's still got time. Maybe he'll show up with someone better," I say.

"I don't think that can be topped," he says, a twinkle in his eye.

"Want to bet on it?"

Chapter 15

Grant

I spot Sean the moment I walk into work the next day.

"Don't even start," he warns.

Was the smile on my face that evident?

"Start what? I was just wondering who gave you a kiss last night? Rachel or the snake."

He jumps on me, trying to put me into a headlock.

"Shut your face," he says and only manages to get my neck because I'm laughing so hard.

"Someone's throwing a hissy fit," I say, and his arm gets tighter. I can't stop, though.

"You cannot tell anyone about this." He's got me good now, so I have to stop laughing to get air.

Johnathon walks in and eyes us. "Isn't it a little early to be fighting over toys?"

"Don't." Sean warns me.

"Sean's dating a snake."

Sean growls and pulls me toward the ground. But I'm still bigger than him. I twist out of his grip and spin until I have him in a headlock.

"You suck."

Mark walks in and looks at the two of us. "Come on guys, let's get to work."

I release Sean.

He straightens, but continues to glare at me. Sean

might be the first to tell the joke, but he's the worst at taking one.

"Sean, I want to take you out to lunch today." Mark says while looking over the daily to-do list.

Sean combs his fingers through his hair, to get it to calm down. "Cool. Where?"

"How about Alfredos? I love their noodles." Boss says it with such seriousness it takes Sean a moment to get it.

"Oh, come on. It was one snake." Sean grunts.

"Yet, you still ran away from it." Lennox says as she walks in.

That right there is the reason for my smile today. I could care less about the snake, but having Lennox hide behind me and bury her face in my back, still has my heart racing.

"I hate you all." Sean grumbles and grabs his bag. He's almost out the door when Michael walks in.

"There's my favorite—"

"Shut up." Sean interrupts him and runs into the shop before any of us can say more.

"Somebody woke up on the wrong side of the den," Michael says, and we all laugh.

This is why I can't lose them. I never had brothers or sisters to joke around with. Everything at my house was so dismal and daunting. Life with the Bentleys is lighthearted and genuine.

"How's the thumb?" Mark turns to me and I notice Lennox standing close enough to hear.

"It's fine. Mostly healed," I respond.

"Just don't overdo it alright? Let the other guys do the hard parts," Mark says and heads to the front of the shop. Michael has already gone out into the shop and it's just me and Lennox left in the staff room.

"So..." She shuffles her feet. "Are you bringing a date to the party?"

She has never asked me questions about my dating life before. I always thought it was because she wasn't interested.

"I haven't decided yet," I say. I wasn't planning on bringing a date, but I also wasn't planning for her to have a boyfriend, either. So it might be an idea worth considering.

Who am I kidding? I don't want to date anyone but her.

"Are you telling me you don't have a little black book with names for days?" she asks.

Is that a hint of jealousy in her voice?

No. It can't be.

She bites her bottom lip. Every time she does that, I just want to taste it myself.

I smile and fold my arms. "Are you interested in reading it?"

"No!" Her cheeks turn pink. My new favorite color. "Of course not."

Then she practically sprints to her office.

Gosh, she's cute. But she's also so much more than that. I pat my chest and the reminder written on my skin. I need to be brave and tell her how I feel. Stop hinting around it and hiding from it, whether or not she has a boyfriend. I can't keep teasing her like this, can't keep holding her at a distance, wishing the space between us would just disappear. I need her.

I take a step in the direction of Lennox's office, but my phone buzzes.

Aunt Megan.

"Hello."

"Oh, Grant," she says like she forgot who she was calling.

"Hi, Megan."

"How are you?" she asks.

"I'm good. I'm working hard."

"Good. That's good." She stalls. "I was, uh, calling to see if you're free on Christmas."

I push back the pain that causes me. I used to dream about having Christmas with my whole family. The mom I never got to meet, a sober dad, my grandpa and my aunt. She did her best to be a mother figure in my life, but that's hard to do when she lives three hours away.

"I don't know," I say.

"Well, if you can swing by, I know your dad would love it."

My scoff cuts her off. "He does not want to see me." And I'm sure he doesn't care to see her either. My aunt and dad never saw eye to eye, and my aunt had her own struggles.

She lets out a breath like she's trying not to cry and I feel guilty. "Time has a way of changing people."

Not people like my dad. But I can't take out my anger against my dad on my aunt. "I'll see what I can do," I say half-heartedly.

"Okay," Megan says. "Well, have a good day."

"You too," I say.

She hangs up, and I expect to feel relief, but I just feel worse. Who's pushing who away? I'm no better than my dad if I can't be brave enough to face him.

I turn on my heel and head toward Mark's office. He's always been the father figure I wish I had. And right now I could use some advice.

He's on the phone when I enter, so I patiently wait by the door.

"Sorry." He hangs up a moment later and smiles at me. "What's up?" Mark asks and pulls a chair over to his computer.

"I wanted to get your advice on something," I say and pull out my phone to the saved listing of the house. "I want to know what you think of this house?"

Mark's eyebrows shoot up. "Let's see." He takes my phone and looks at everything from the square footage to the bathroom light fixtures.

"This is a great price per square foot," he says and begins listing all the excellent features of the house. "My only concern is the settling in that area. In the past, they didn't lay the foundation correctly and the houses around there sunk."

"Oh." I fall back in my seat, watching my dream crash before my eyes.

"But it looks to be on the newer end." He hands the phone back. "Why don't I make a few calls and then we'll go out there with a house inspector and check it out."

My mouth drops. "Wha—No. I can't make you do that."

"Son, I'd be honored to go along with you. My kids don't seem to have the same drive as you do. You've always worked hard for yourself and I'm proud of you."

My eyes burn, but I sniff back the pain. "Thank you."

"Anytime, son."

I leave his office, feeling lighter than I have in years. Maybe I was wrong to assume I wasn't a part of the family. Maybe I always have been.

Five hours later, I'm even more convinced of this.

Mark managed to get us and an inspector into the house, where we discovered the settling was no longer an issue, and I fell even more in love with the house. He then got on the phone with the realtor and by the end of the work day we'd submitted an offer.

I don't hear anything back until the next day.

"Grant!" Mark hollers from the front of the shop.

I drop what I'm doing and run inside. "Yeah, boss?" I feel like a kid on Christmas. Please tell me Santa delivered.

His face breaks into a smile. "You got the house."

"What?"

"You did it, son." He wraps me in a hug and this time I do cry. I have a house. Well, not for thirty days, and an extra month or two of renovations.

"Now, let's address the money issue. I'd like to offer you a low-interest loan."

My jaw drops and my legs turn to jelly. I drop into a chair and stare at him.

He's done so much for me. Welcoming me into his house, helping me find my own, and now this? It's too much.

"I can't take your money."

He laughs. "You do every two weeks. This wouldn't be much different."

He's got a point there. "How much are we talking?" I never wanted to be indebted to someone, but who better to be indebted to than a Bentley?

We discuss how much I've saved, and what the loan would entail for the next hour, and Mark turns everyone away to focus on me. He runs a tight ship in the shop, but he is also the most giving man I've ever met.

I want to be just like him.

"Thank you, Mark," I say, finally standing from my chair.

"There's nothing I love more than seeing my kids happy." He pats me on the shoulder. "And something tells me you're going to be very happy in that house."

An image of Lennox floats to mind. "I think I am too."

Chapter 16

Lennox

I barely saw Grant at work today, and when I did, he seemed distracted. He was in and out of my dad's office all day yesterday, and when I asked my dad about it, he just shrugged and said I'd find out.

I've been waiting for Grant to get home ever since. It's six now. My parents are out on their weekly date and ever since Michael got engaged, he hasn't been over as often to watch romance movies with me.

I can't take the silence anymore. I sit down on my favorite spot on the couch, flip on a Korean drama, and pull out my book.

One of these days, I'll actually watch the show, but for now, all I need is the steady hum of the TV, so I can drift effortlessly into a fictional world. I used to think I could write my own stories, but then I nearly failed all of my high school English classes and I gave up on that idea. I aced digital art class though, and that's when my love for graphic design began. In May, I'll graduate and I'll start my own business to illustrate the stories other people can dream up. Which I can do whenever and wherever I want as soon as I find customers.

I flip open my new romance novel to the first page and am fully invested by page thirty and can't stop reading. I'm a princess of some obscure European country, preparing to take the throne, but first I must

find love. All goes well, as well as any true romance can go, until I get locked in the vault with the Crown Jewels. Traitors of the throne are here to steal everything valuable in the castle, me included. There's a loud bang against the vault door, then—
Boom!
"Ahhh!" I scream and throw my book across the room.
Grant watches with amusement from the opposite couch.
When did he get here?
"What just happened?" I shout at him, still trying to calm my racing heart after nearly being kidnapped and killed by fictional bad guys. Where's my book boyfriend when I need him?
"A bomb went off," he says with a little laugh, pointing at the TV.
It's no longer playing a foreign drama, but rather an old war film.
I take that back. It's worse. It's a documentary.
"You changed my show?"
"I wanted to see if you'd notice. It took you forty-five minutes, by the way."
He's been sitting there for forty-five minutes? Please don't tell me I picked my nose or something.
"Well, now you can turn it off." I say.
He laughs and pauses the show. Thank heavens.
"What if I said there is a love story in it?" he asks.
I raise an eyebrow. "I still wouldn't watch it."
"Why? It's just like one of those chick flicks you read. Except you can actually learn something from this."
My mouth drops open. "I'm so offended by all the words that just came out of your mouth. Who says you

can't learn anything from a romance novel?"

His head falls back, and he laughs. "Like what? That Prince Charming is always right around the corner?"

I shake my head slowly. "I didn't know you were such a cynic."

His smile fades a little. "Consider me a realist."

A realist who needs to learn a lesson. "I need to go to the bathroom. Why don't you skip to the romance scenes in this...documentary." I shudder at the word.

"I knew you'd come around."

I press my lips together to hide my smile. "Mm hmm." Instead of going to the bathroom, I raid the mess room. We can no longer do slime in the house for obvious reasons. But water pranks haven't been restricted, yet.

I grab some pop rocks and a balloon, then go to the kitchen to get us some drinks. Two cokes and a coconut water for Grant after he finds my prank. No one in my family even likes coconut water, but there's always a few in the fridge just for Grant. If that doesn't make it clear he's part of the family, I don't know what would.

Except, maybe a gold band on his left ring finger that matches the one on mine.

I grab the drinks, sticking the coconut water behind my back for now.

"Want a drink?" I ask, sitting down beside him this time.

Crap, now I'm in the splash zone.

I consider moving, but it's too late.

"Thanks." He pushes play, then reaches for the coke. "Wait, did you do something to it?"

"Why would I do something to your drink?" I ask, nonchalantly, sitting back in my seat.

He eyes the coke as if he's searching for clues.

"Because you grew up with three brothers. And the cap has been opened."

Darn it. I knew he wouldn't fall for it.

He twists open the lid and sniffs it. "What is that? Pepper?"

I shrug. "And maybe some pop rocks."

"Nice try."

I sigh and reach behind me for his stupid coconut water. "Fine. Here you go."

"Thank you." He smiles and tips his water toward me, then leans back in his seat.

I can't even concentrate on the show. I keep sneaking peeks at Grant, who seems to be thoroughly entertained. What's even going on? And why are they just talking?

So. Much. Talking.

My coke is almost gone by the time Grant finally lifts his coconut water for a drink. He keeps his eyes on the screen as he cracks open the lid. I watch him remove the cap and jump out of the way when the water sprays out.

"Agh!" Grant bolts up, water dripping down his face. "What the—Lennox!"

Crap. I was too busy laughing to run away.

I jump over the back of the couch with a squeal. He's right behind me. I try to zig zag but catch the corner of the rug and Grant rams into the back of me. I lose my balance and we both fall together, then roll to a stop under the Christmas tree.

This time, he's on top of me. I stop breathing, but not just because he's on my diaphragm.

"You got me." His voice is oddly gruff and overly attractive.

"You said I couldn't learn anything from a romance novel, so I had to prove you wrong." I breathe.

"Pranks?"

I bite my lip, and his gaze drops to my mouth.

"To take advantage of every moment." My words drop off as the look in his eyes grows more intense.

His head drops and I can almost taste his minty breath on my lips.

I'm more than ready to close that distance and get a taste of my first kiss. I'm not scared of that hungry look in his eyes because it mirrors mine. I want this kiss. I need him—

Crash!

Grant's body protects me from the tree's branches again, but not even his impeccable muscles can save my mom's one-of-a-kind glass ornaments from shattering on the wood floor.

"Devil tree." Grant mutters as he pushes himself and the tree back to a standing position.

I agree, but my mom won't. Thank heavens she and my dad are still out on a date.

Grant starts putting the tree back together and I do my best to help, but we've lost too many decorations.

"Dang it." Grant mutters as he looks at the pathetic thing.

"It doesn't look too bad." I say, angling my head to the left, then to the right. Neither direction helps.

Grant turns and heads for the door.

"Where are you going?"

"To the store to buy more ornaments." He says, barely stopping long enough to put shoes on.

I yank on my own and follow him out the door. He won't know where to get those kinds of ornaments without me.

Turns out, he doesn't need me. There are only a few options left in the store, and they are all hideous.

"Purple or orange?" Grant asks.

"Neither." My mom's tree is red and gold.

He sighs and walks away from the options. "My grandpa used to put candy canes on the tree," he says wistfully.

"That's a great idea." I agree with him, and we pick out no less than fifty red and white striped candy canes. Then we walk casually through the aisles, joking about what we could cover the tree with. Kitchen utensils, toilet paper, loofahs.

"Wait." I stop by the photo section and pick up some small frame ornaments. "I have an idea."

Three years ago, my mom scanned all our childhood photos and saved them online. There are thousands. Tons of Christmas photos, but even better, they're photos no one wanted to be taken.

It's almost nine by the time we get back to the house, ready to redecorate the tree with candy canes and embarrassing photos.

"Where should we put Sean's broken nose from his first girlfriend?" I ask Grant.

"Front and center."

Michael's headgear comes next, then the photo of mom when she tried to be brunette for the summer. Think regular Cheetos plus hot Cheetos.

"My favorite one," Grant says, putting another picture ornament on the tree. I round the tree and look at it.

"I did not print that one!" I reach for the awful photo of myself, but Grant stops me.

"I added it to the cart when you weren't looking." He says and pins my arms against my sides when I try to grab it again.

"That is not going on the tree. It's terrifying." I try to wiggle free, but I'm firmly stuck against his chest. Guess I'm staying here forever. His evil plan backfired.

"I kind of liked your goth stage." He laughs and points to the choker necklace I wore in the picture. "I think you look cute."

My goth stage lasted exactly three days, but somehow there are over seventy pictures trying to prove otherwise.

"I was not cute."

He spins me around in his arm until I'm pressed up against his chest. "I've always thought you were beautiful."

Whoa… hold on. What?

"Me?" I squeak.

His smile isn't teasing anymore. It's serious. Has he ever looked at me like this before?

"Lennox?" he whispers.

"Yes?" I breathe.

"Are you still dating Noa?"

Noa who? Dating? These words don't even make sense. How do I explain what Noa and I are? The party is tomorrow but I don't know if I can hold out for one more day. I don't know if I want to.

"What happened to my tree?" My mother asks, and Grant and I jump apart.

I tear my eyes away from him. Will he hate me after the work party tomorrow?

I force a smile for my mom. "We upgraded it."

Chapter 17

Lennox

I tug on the front of my black dress and it becomes too revealing, so I pull it back. Now I'm a nun. What do I do with this weird cut-out neckline? Juliet helped me pick it out, just for tonight, but I'm already regretting it.

Noa studies me, his eyes growing more worried every time I fidget with my dress. "Are you ready?"

"What? Yeah. Of course." I pull at my dress again. "Why wouldn't I be?"

His left brow arches. "Because we've been standing outside for fifteen minutes."

Right. That. "Has it really been that long?"

"It's really been that long," he says gently. "Do you want to run through the plan again?"

"Yes. Let's do that." I join him by one of the pillars in front of my parent's house he's apparently been leaning against for the last fourteen minutes. "So…the plan." What's the plan? I forgot the plan!

Noa grabs my hands. "Relax." He rubs small circles on the back of my hand and I remind myself to breathe. "We're just going to go in there, have dinner, show your brothers you've won, and then announce that we're engaged. Then we will have a stupid fight about nothing and I'll leave you heartbroken."

Right. Yes. So easy. Just a little, "Hey guys, I'm engaged, but not really."

"What if they see right through it?"

Noa smiles and points to his face. "With these puppy dog eyes aimed at you all night? How can they not believe it?"

He has a point. Those are some pretty convincing puppy dog eyes. I've never seen anything like that on Grant, which means...nothing. Because I don't want him to be jealous. I want him to want me of course, but not because I'm with someone else. But my brothers, what if they're ticked?

"I don't know if I can do this. I've never been a good liar," I admit.

"Just think of it as a play. We are putting on a show for a few hours, then it's done. And you can come clean whenever you want."

I nod. But it must seem like I need more convincing because he goes on.

"I'm not your fiancé. Think of me as a playmate." His face goes red, and my laughter dispels all the stress mounting in my body. "That didn't come out right." He's got a sheepish smile on his face and it's my new favorite expression.

"It was effective though." I laugh. "I think I'm ready to go in now."

"Oh, wait." He pauses and starts digging in his pocket. He pulls something out and holds it in his hands. "I just wanted to say thank you. For coming with me to the reunion, and for showing me what a true friend is."

He places a small object in my hand: a ring with a dainty little star on top. "And I don't want you to forget how important you are. Even if the people around you forget to remind you, know that you're amazing."

My vision goes blurry, and I pull him in for a hug.

"Noa. This is so sweet. Thank you." In two weeks, this man beside me went from a stranger to a fake fiancé, to a friend, and, well, back to a fake fiancé. I couldn't be more grateful for him. "Promise you won't ditch me after whatever happens tonight?" I half laugh, half cry.

"No way. I already signed you up for karaoke next week."

I pull back with a laugh. "Of course you did." I look at the ring in my hand again. I suppose it will work as a pretend engagement ring. Except it's huge.

"Noa, what size did you get?" I laugh. The only finger it fits on is my thumb, and it's still too big.

He scratches the back of his head. "There are sizes?"

"Oh dear, please come to me before you propose to some beautiful girl with a bracelet."

He shrugs. "What if she likes bracelets?"

"Noa."

"Kidding." But he's wearing a mischievous grin and I'm pretty sure he's still contemplating this idea.

Don't worry, future wife of Noa Reid, I've got you.

I take a deep breath and face the door again. "Alright. Let's do this."

Noa opens the door, and we step inside.

Five feet in, and I want to run back out. Six feet in, and I'm pretty sure I just entered another universe. Ten feet in, and I know this night is about to get crazy.

Chapter 18

Lennox

"Huge Ice tree," Noa says, looking at the monstrosity in front of us. "I have so many questions."

"Don't we all," I say, staring at the seven-foot Christmas tree, carved chunk of ice, looming over the party guests. There are branches and ornaments, even presents at the base. I don't even want to imagine the amount of money my dad wasted on this. It's frozen water, for crying out loud!

"Pumpkin." My dad appears behind the giant tree sculpture and rounds it to give me a hug. "This must be your date."

"Noa." My giant of a date sticks out his hand. "Pleasure to meet you."

My dad gives me a not-so-hidden grin. "I like him."

What do I say to that? Thanks? I picked him out myself?

"Dad, I have two questions." I say. "Why the big ice tree? And please tell me my Christmas bonus is not in that thing."

My dad only laughs. "My daughter is a keeper," he says to Noa, then runs off to talk to more people. Sometimes, I forget that there are fifteen other employees that work at the shop beside my brothers. I'm rarely around all the guys, so being here with them and their dates is a little nerve-wracking. And where are my brothers? And Grant?

We make our way through the crowd toward the food table, but Juliet catches us.

"Hey! Oh my gosh, you're here!" She says to Noa.

Noa winks at her in return. "Nowhere else I'd rather be."

"Oh." Juliet looks at me with wide eyes. "He's good. This is going to work."

"Speaking of the devils, where are they?" I ask, but not ready for the answer. I'm not ready to pretend to be engaged.

"Right this way." She has an eager gleam in her eye.

I worry it's because she's keeping secrets from everyone. Big, dark, life-changing secrets.

Or, she's just super chill and nice.

"You didn't tell Michael, did you?" I ask her.

"And risk seeing the look on his face? No way." She practically cackles as she leads us to the kitchen where Grant and my brothers are snacking on hors d'oeuvres.

"Hey guys, look who I found by the door," Juliet says to the group.

Four heads turn in my direction. Three of them look at me with amusement in their eyes, but the one on the left, with the dark features and a scar through his eyebrow, has never looked at me like that. Like he's devouring every inch of me. My body heats under his interested gaze.

Is this plan working?

"Hey!" Michael is the first to greet Noa. The rest have already met him and don't seem as eager. "You brought a date, Lenny. I didn't think you had it in you."

My blood boils, but before I can retort, Noa covers my hand with his large one.

"You underestimate your sister." Noa says, then looks down at me with admiration in his eyes. "You don't know how amazing she is."

My cheeks are surely red as tomatoes, but I appreciate it more than he knows.

I feel Grant's gaze on me, and it pulls my attention to him. His brows are furrowed and his arms folded. He looks angry. I almost pull my hand from Noa's, but I'm not done with my brothers yet and I need Noa's support.

"She's alright." Sean chuckles.

Dad calls us over for the end-of-year "you guys were incredible" speech, and then we get food. Noa protects me on one side, but somehow Grant ends up in the other seat beside me, and that's worse than one of my obnoxious brothers. I've sat beside him multiple times at family dinner, but I've never been so aware of every move he makes.

"So are you dating?" Michael asks from across the large banquet style table.

Noa squeezes my shoulder. "Something like that."

"Really?" Trent hedges. "I haven't seen Lennox date a guy for years."

I swallow my last bite of food and force a smile onto my lips, looking up lovingly at Noa. "I guess it just took the right guy."

Grant clears his throat beside me and I shoot him a look, but he's not looking at me. Just gripping his fork like he's trying to wring the life out of it.

This isn't working.

"I guess we owe her some money." Trent says, then looks at me. "Oh shoot, you did tell him, didn't you?"

My hand shakes as I try to pretend I'm immune to their teasing. "Of course I told my fiancé about your stupid bet."

It takes exactly two point five seconds before it registers. Grant reacts first. Then Michael, then the twins. "What did you just say?" Grant barks and the entire party goes silent.

Noa squeezes my hand.

I paste on a brave smile for my brothers. "I have to thank you guys, actually. Without this little bet, I never would have met the love of my life."

Noa smiles down at me, but all I'm aware of is how hot it is in here. Shouldn't a giant ice sculpture cool things down?

"No," Michael says. He stands up, and so do the rest of them. "No way."

My three brothers turn toward Noa as if they can scare him off with their presence, but he's got a foot in each direction on all of them and he stands up to prove it.

"Lennox, you're not serious," Trent says, looking down at me.

I don't like this vantage point, so I push my chair back and stand up.

I frown at them, purposely ignoring Grant's heated gaze. It looks much more fierce than it did last night. I swallow despite the nerves creeping up my back. "I'm more serious than I've ever been about anything."

"This is a joke, Lennox." Michael laughs awkwardly.

"No, it's not." I'm one second away from stomping my foot like a toddler.

My brothers are each wearing a different version of the same glare they inherited from my dad. But my brief bout of victory is dimmed by Grant's deep frown.

"We're actually going to Vegas over Christmas." I say. I never told Noa this part, and his grip tightens.

"No, you're not." It's Grant this time, and every hair on the back of my neck stands on end. Does he hate me right now? Or could he actually be jealous?

"Dad!" Sean shouts. "You can't let her do this."

Dad shrugs and gives me a side hug. "I think my little girl is big enough to make her own decisions."

"I don't believe this." Michael shoves his hands through his hair, and the veins in Grant's neck are bulging. Sean, to his credit, just looks amused. "I'm not letting you go anywhere with him," Michael says.

Grant steps up beside him with folded arms. "Me neither."

Trent nods in agreement, and Sean does as well.

I narrow my eyes, eyeing each one of them. "I'm either invisible or the butt of every joke to you guys. And I'm so sick of it. You guys don't control my life."

During my rant, Noa dropped my hand and steadied me around the waist, which only made my brothers angrier.

"We're just protecting you, Len," Trent says.

I shake my head. I really didn't want it to get this heated, but hey, free entertainment for the rest of the guests. Too bad Sean didn't bring his snake date to take off some of the heat. "I don't need protection. I just need someone on my side."

"Like him?" Grant nods toward Noa.

I finally look up at Noa to see how he's taking all of this. He's not running for the hills, which is good.

"He's seen more in me in the last two weeks than any of you have for my whole life." I say.

Grant falls back a step like I've struck him. "That's not true," he whispers.

A tear slips down my cheek, and I swipe it away.

I look back at my brothers, reminding myself who this prank is really on. "There's nothing you can do to change my mind. I'm marrying Noa." The words are sticky in my throat and I barely get them out.

"I don't get it." Sean says. "You haven't dated anyone for years and now you're getting married to a guy you've only known for fourteen days?"

Kudos to Sean for picking out the one flaw in my plan.

I shoot Juliet a look, but she looks as lost as I feel.

"Love doesn't follow a timeline." *Wow, that was cheesy, even for me.*

Sean seems to consider it. "Well, if you're really in love, you won't mind that you're standing under the mistletoe."

My chin lifts in slow motion. There it is. I thought mistletoe only showed up in inconvenient places in Hallmark movies.

I look at Noa, silently begging him to fix this. But how?

I'm keenly aware of just how many people are watching us, waiting for us to do something that should be so natural for an engaged couple. But it's not natural for me, and my heart picks up speed.

I look at Grant and the jealousy in his eyes is what I'd convinced myself I wanted. So why doesn't it feel good?

"Come here, muffin." Noa tugs me closer. "It's been too long since I kissed you last." He smiles down at me, trying to calm me like he did before we got on that stage. But it's not working this time.

His head drops and I fight everything in me to not pull away.

It's not like it'll be a real kiss. It's just for the prank. We're playing a part.

I close my eyes and count to ten. I only make it to five before a hand falls on my arm and I'm ripped away from Noa.

I stagger back and look up. "Grant? What are you doing?"

"You're not marrying him," he says, his voice low and husky.

It's eerily quiet.

"I knew it," Noa says, and I look back at him. "I knew you were in love with him."

I'm so thrown by the turn of events that I barely register that this is part of the plan to make my brothers feel bad.

I step away from Grant and reach for Noa but he backs away. "Noa, wait."

"No." He holds up a giant hand. "I get it. I thought I could swoop you away before he realized what he was missing, but you didn't deserve that."

Wow, he's good.

"But what about us?" A tear slips down my cheek, and boy, it feels real. I must be getting the hang of this acting thing.

Noa offers me a sad smile. "I think we both knew there was never an us." With that, he turns and walks away.

It's so quiet. The eyes of everyone I know and don't know are on me. I want to laugh, because how else do you handle the end of a fake relationship?

Instead, I turn and glare at my brothers. "Are you happy now? Do you see what your bets have done?"

They each looked shocked by my accusation. "I'm

sorry, Lennox." Trent says and drops his head.

"I hope you are. Someone deserves to be." I turn and run from the house, pretending I'm holding back tears, but it's not until I reach the gazebo that I let out the laugh that's been bubbling up for hours.

That felt good.

Chapter 19

Grant

Lennox was engaged.

Now she's not.

That's all it takes to get my legs working and sprinting after her. I thought I heard someone cheer when the front door closed behind me, but my mind is solely on Lennox. She ripped my heart right out of my chest when she announced she was engaged to Noa. But now I have a chance again. I'll take it slow. As slow as she needs. But I won't risk losing her again.

She was wrong when she said no one saw her.

All I see is her. Even when she thinks she's invisible, I see her. How she's always drawing on her tablet or reading a romance novel, loves to bake, and hates the color green. Which is weird, but I love that about her. The way she stops and talks to any old lady we pass on the street. It's like she's a magnet for them, a beacon of hope and happiness. At least, she always has been for me.

I slowly approach the gazebo. She must be sad, even if her failed engagement thrills me.

But she's not crying. Is she…laughing?

"Lennox?"

She jumps, and her phone skids across the floor of the gazebo.

I lean over and pick it up. The screen lights up with

a text from Noa. Acid washes over my skin at the sight of his name. But then I see the four little words that turn the entire night upside down.
Noa: Did they buy it?
"Thanks." Lennox grabs the phone and turns away from me.
What did that mean? Did who buy what? The engagement? Or the break-up? Or both?
I was so livid when she broke the news that she was engaged, I couldn't see straight, but in hindsight, her story was full of holes. They didn't act like they were in love. I mean, they tried, but if I had been in Noa's place, I wouldn't have hesitated to kiss her under the mistletoe. I would have been kissing her all night.
Was this whole thing a joke on me and her brothers?
Dang. She wins the Bentley prank cup for sure, if that's the case. There's only one way to find out.
"Are you okay?" I ask, stepping up next to her along the rail.
She turns her face away before shaking her head. But I saw her tear free cheeks.
"You must have really been in love," I say, egging her on. If I push enough, she'll crack, but after what she put me through tonight, she deserves a little pressure.
She nods.
I choose my next words carefully. "I can talk to him, if you want. Clear up the misunderstanding."
Her head flips in my direction, her eyes wide and afraid. "What?"
I bite back the smile brimming on my lips. "Unless…you weren't really in love with him."
"Of course I was." She defends herself, but I don't

miss the slight twitch in the left corner of her lip. It's always been her tell. Each of the Bentley siblings has a tell, but not one of them will admit they are wrong until proven. And I'm not stopping until she admits just how wrong she was.

I nod and take a step closer. "And you were going to get married to him. In Vegas?"

"Y-yes." She swallows, then shivers.

"But you've never kissed him?"

She starts to nod, then stops.

I got her.

"I think you were scared to kiss him."

She snorts. "No, I wasn't."

"You were terrified," I say, just like I did, six years ago in this very spot.

Her lips part, but no words come out. She shivers again, and I shrug off my jacket and drape it around her shoulders.

I want to kiss her, but only when she's ready.

I place a hand on her waist and tug her into me, and she lets out a soft gasp. Her amber eyes widen, and nearby lights reflect off her irises. "You should never let anyone kiss you unless you want them to," I whisper.

She bites her lips, and I force myself to stay put. For a few more seconds.

"I've never wanted anyone to kiss me but you." The words are a breathy admission.

I freeze . "You've never been kissed?" But more importantly, she wants me to kiss her?

She shakes her head and tugs at the top of her dress, and her bracelets tinkle against each other. "I think I'm more than ready for my first kiss."

If that's not permission, I don't know what is. I drop

my head slowly. Her eyes fall shut and her head tips back.

"Your first kiss should mean something," I whisper.

I brush my lips against her cheek and she leans into it.

"And when you're ready..." I press my lips to her ear, then back along her jaw, tracing my way to her mouth. "You take advantage of the moment." I hover over her lips.

She grabs two fistfuls of my shirt and tugs me to her, melding our lips together. I kiss her soft and slow, letting her find her way through it. I tug on her lip and she wraps her arms around my neck.

Why haven't I spent the last six years kissing her like this?

I pull back, "It was a good prank."

She looks up at me with glassy eyes. "It's not a prank anymore."

Chapter 20

Grant

I take Lennox's hand as we walk back to the house. I don't care if her brothers give us crap. Let them throw foam balloons and shoot the confetti cannons. I'll take it all for her.

My phone buzzes in my pocket, but I silence it.

A snowflake falls on my nose, and I pull Lennox to a stop in front of the house. "Wait," I whisper, pointing to the cloud-covered sky.

She looks up as snow begins to fall around us. Tiny snowflakes drift silently to the earth, and the world is calm and quiet. She tilts her head back, enjoying the rare beauty of snow in Arizona.

The snow is nothing compared to the beauty in front of me. I brush the blonde strands back from her face and lean in to kiss her. I pause right before our lips touch.

"I've always seen you, Lennox," I whisper. "All I see is you."

Her eyelashes flutter, and she bites her bottom lip again. "Really?"

I nod. "I'm sorry I acted like your annoying brother for so long."

She touches my chin. "I've never seen you as my brother."

She leans in and my phone buzzes again.

"You should get that," she whispers against my lips.

I sigh and step back, reaching for my phone. A name pops up, and it stops the blood in my veins.

Dad.

My shoulders and chest turn to ice. Do I answer it? He hasn't called in years. What could he want?

"Answer it." Lennox nudges my arm.

My thumb twitches as I slide it across the screen. "Hello?"

"Hi." My father's rough voice crackles through the phone. When was the last time I heard his voice? "Hello." He says again. "I've uh, been meaning to call you."

I kick a pebble off the sidewalk. He couldn't have picked a worse time.

"Okay," I say, waiting for him to continue.

"I'm in the hospital."

Whatever I expected him to say, it wasn't that.

"Are you okay?" I hate how worried I feel when he's never been concerned about me.

"I'm sick. It's liver disease…and it doesn't look good. I know how you feel about me, but I just wanted you to know."

"What?" I breathe.

"I know I'm the last person you want to see," he coughs a few times before continuing. "But I'd like to apologize to you in person."

Apologize in person? How sick is he? I didn't expect to feel fear, or worry for him, but it's still there, in the middle of my chest like an ax.

I swallow the lump in my throat. "Where are you?"

He tells me which hospital and mumbles directions of where to find him, but my mind is running.

After all of this. After all he's done to me, after all the pain he caused me, can I forgive him just because he's sick?

I hang up.

"What's wrong?" Lennox asks. She grabs my hand and pulls me closer.

I rub at my chest, and the pinpricks of pain spread. "My dad is in the hospital."

"Let's go," she says.

I finally look at her. "We?"

"Yes." She nods. "I'm coming with you. Give me your keys."

My emotions are all over the place, but the feelings I have for this girl are the only thing keeping me standing right now.

The drive flies by, and before I'm ready, the hospital comes into view.

Once we get inside, I can barely move. Lennox takes my hand and leads me through the hospital. She stops and talks to a woman behind a desk, but I don't register what they say.

What can I say to the man who spent my entire life drinking instead of remembering he had a kid? Sorry karma caught up to you?

Okay, so clearly I haven't forgiven and forgotten just because he's sick.

"His room is just down this hall," Lennox says, nudging me forward, but I feel like I'm trudging through wet cement. My lungs aren't letting enough air into my body.

We come to a small waiting room, and I collapse into the first chair I see. Dropping my head into my hands, I focus on taking deep breaths.

In.... Out.... In....

"Grant? Are you okay?" she asks, her words so soft I

almost miss them.

I drag a hand through my hair, which I'm sure is standing on end right now. "Not really."

She doesn't respond right away, and the silence finally gives me courage to open up to someone for the first time. "I was never honest with you guys about my family." I swallow the emotions working their way up. "I never knew my mom. According to my dad, she never wanted to be a mom. All I had was my dad and grandpa until my grandpa passed away. Grandpa pretty much raised me, while my dad spent his days drinking and his nights yelling."

She doesn't speak, for which I'm grateful. She places a steadying hand on my back, and I go on.

"I moved out the second I turned eighteen. I couldn't live with him anymore."

"What?" She grabs my arm hard and I finally look at her. "You turned eighteen in January of your senior year. Where did you go?"

I give her a half-smile. "To that apartment."

Tears spring from her amber eyes like someone just opened the waterway. I guess I did.

"You've been living on your own, in that place since you were in high school?" She doesn't give me time to respond. "Why didn't you say anything? You know my parents would have let you stay with us. I can't believe you've been there all this time."

I lift my fingers to her cheek and wipe away her tears, gathering them one by one, appreciating her empathy.

"You know me. I don't accept help very well. And I was too ashamed to admit my reasons for leaving. I thought I wasn't man enough to stay there. I'd only ever been a disappointment to my dad. My aunt kept an eye on me, though."

She shakes her head and my hand falls from her cheek. "That's not enough. You didn't deserve that. You deserve a family who loves and adores you. Like mine does."

Something kicks me right in the chest. Like her family does? Or like she does?

"Thanks to you, I ended up there, eventually."

She swipes at her remaining tears and forces a smile. I can see in her eyes she wants to ask more questions, but she leaves those things behind for now. For me.

"Do you want to go in?"

I look away and shake my head. "I don't know if I can."

"I understand that," she says, then after a moment, she speaks up again. "But will you regret it if you don't?"

Yes. She knows the answer to that, or she never would have asked the question.

"I know the last thing you want to be is your dad, so if you can, be the man you always wished your father would be."

I pat my chest where my tattoo sits. She's right. Ignoring my dad in his time of need would make me no better than him. But I don't want to do it alone.

"Will you come in with me?" I ask and then regret it. That's the last place she probably wants to be.

"Of course." Lennox stands and holds out a hand to me. I take it and let her pull me up. Once we are standing, she doesn't let go, and neither do I. She's the steady presence that I need to see this through.

When we reach the door, she gives my hand a

squeeze and pulls me in.

Chapter 21

Grant

I don't know what I expect to see when I walk into the sterile hospital room, but it's not my dad and aunt Megan happily talking. They never got along while I was growing up.

"Grant." Megan jumps out of her chair and rushes to me. She pulls me into a hug, and Lennox starts to pull her hand free, but I hold it tight.

I still need her.

"I didn't know you were coming," Megan says as she pulls away.

"I didn't know either," I admit. I turn to Lennox. "This is Lennox, Lennox, my Aunt Megan." I say.

Lennox steps forward and gives Megan a hug. "So nice to meet you."

"Grant," my father says from the bed, and I look at him. When did he get so old? He's barely fifty but he looks twenty years older than that, and his skin is sunken and yellow.

"Dad." I swallow. "How long have you been sick?" I hear myself ask.

My dad blinks and looks away. "For longer than I've wanted to admit."

Lennox squeezes my hand, sensing my need for her. I guess I've always needed her more than she knows.

"I brought this on myself." My dad's voice cracks,

and all kinds of broken pieces of my heart start beating again. "You deserve a lot more from me than I ever gave you. Maybe I can offer an explanation."

I open my mouth, but he cuts me off.

"I know an explanation doesn't take away the years of pain you suffered. But that's about all I can offer you now."

I turn to Lennox. "You can leave, if you want."

She looks up at me, completely unafraid, like this is just another prank we're about to pull on her brothers. "I don't want to leave."

My heart bursts with love for this woman at my side. I've given her every out I can think of, but she hasn't left. I nod and pull Lennox closer to the bed. We take a seat and wait.

Megan sits back down in her chair, and then Dad speaks. "I wanted to be a good dad to you. But I was so angry at your mother for leaving us like she did. I let that anger fester until I couldn't handle it anymore. So I started drinking to numb the pain."

Dad sniffs, and the man in front of me is not the father I grew up with. This man is real and human.

"I was always so grateful my father took over caring for you. I'd see you two together, and you both looked so much happier without me."

My hand clenches around Lennox's. "All I wanted was a father who actually cared about me."

He nods, and tears drip down his cheeks. "I was so lost to my addiction, I forgot about you. Addiction is a funny thing like that. It might take away your pain, but it just adds that pain to someone else's." He pauses and his breath comes heavy. I wait for him to continue. "The more I drank the worse I felt. So I drank more. It was a never-ending cycle, and you were the victim."

I sniff and scratch at my nose.

"It took waking up to a death sentence to set me free this time." My dad says with a rough exhale.

My head and my heart are at war. I want to be angry at him forever, but when has being angry ever fixed anything?

"I don't expect you to ever forgive me," Dad says. "I know I don't deserve it. But I needed you to know that it was never you. The only problem was me." Tears stream down my father's sallow cheeks and one drips from my own. "I'm so sorry."

Those three little words soften my heart, and I find myself leaning over the bed to hug the man I spent so many years hiding from.

"I want to make it right, son," my dad says. "I won't be here for long, but I want to spend whatever time I have left making it up to you."

I nod into my dad's shoulder. I know I can't instantly forgive him, but I can at least give him that.

"I'll be here," I say, surprised by how much I mean it. Not just because he's sick, but because I've always wanted my father back, and now I have him. If only for a moment.

I release my father and sit back down by Lennox who reaches for my hand again. I slide mine into hers. This feels so good.

Why did I let the rejection ingrained in me ruin my chances at happiness? Every relationship I entered, I kept myself safe by keeping one foot out the door before I could be shoved out. But only the good things in life were worth the risk of stepping all the way in and shutting the door behind me.

Had I let myself do that sooner, I could have been holding Lennox's hand for the last six years.

"You're the Bentley's daughter, right?" My aunt Megan asks Lennox.

"Yeah." She smiles at my aunt and dad without judgment. She knows my history, and she's still looking at my family like she's always known them. Lennox is just that way. She never judges others. Instead, she sees them without negativity, without a filter. She's special like that.

My aunt grins at us. "With how much Grant used to talk about you when I came to visit, I knew he had a crush on you. I'm glad you two are together."

Chapter 22

Lennox

What did his aunt just say?

Will Grant deny it? Because I really don't want him to. I want it to be real. I want everything with Grant to be real.

Grant's hand loosens in mine, but I hold it tighter. Now might be my only chance to come clean.

"I always had a crush on him too," I say.

Grant turns to look at me and my face heats up.

"I'm glad he was always welcome with your family." His dad says, his eyes glistening with tears. My heart breaks for him. It took him years of suffering to recognize his mistakes. Everyone makes their own choices in life. He let Grant go, but that's not a mistake I'm willing to make.

I can tell that out of everything Grant went through, this is the thing that's going to take the longest to forgive. How does one handle not being wanted?

I can only hope that when I tell him I want him, he believes me. But for right now, I should let him have some space. He could use some time without me present to patch things up with his dad.

"I'm going to go, and let you guys catch up," I say, standing up and disengaging my hand from his.

He looks up at me with fear in his eyes.

"Call me and I'll be back," I say. "I need to get home

before my family gets worried."

He nods, seeming to remember the events from the last hour. He stands up with me, taking my hand again. "I'll be right back," he says to his dad and leads me from the room. He's silent as we walk, and I wait until we reach the car before I speak.

"Are you going to be okay?"

He scrubs his free hand down his face and lets out an exhausted breath. "I think so."

I squeeze his hand before letting go. Now that we're outside, I should give him distance. This is new territory for us, and he's already been through a lot tonight.

"So uh," he lets out a breath. "Was what you said in there true?"

I only said a few things, so I know exactly which one he's talking about. "Yes." I bite my fingernail. "Painfully true."

His eyebrows furrow. "Why did you hide your crush on me?"

I scoff. "Are you kidding? You were two grades above me, and best friends with all my brothers. I had to keep my feelings quiet, or I'd never be let anywhere near you."

He nods. "That's true."

"Why didn't *you* say anything?" I ask.

He tucks a strand of hair behind my ear, and my cheeks warm. "Because I watched them chase off every guy. Helped them even. I thought for sure that if I ever made a move, they'd chase me off too."

"Good thing I took care of them." I smile up at him. Speaking of, my brothers still don't know it was all a joke. I should probably tell them.

"I always knew you had it in you," he whispers.

His tongue grazes across his bottom lip, and I follow its course. His head drops toward my own. I close my eyes, aching to feel his lips on mine again. I've always been so scared to kiss someone. Scared that I would mess it up somehow, but this is Grant. He's never scared me.

His lips touch mine. So soft I shouldn't feel anything, but I do. My heart races, and my pulse throbs. I don't have to think. I don't have to try. My lips react to him in the way they were always meant to.

He pulls back. "I'm sorry."

I blink, trying to clear the fog in my brain. "W-what?"

He shakes his head and backs away. "I'm sorry for bringing you into my crap. You'd be better off with someone else. Someone like Noa."

"Why?"

He looks up like my question confuses him. "Why what?"

"Why would you think I would ever be better off without you?"

He sniffs and looks back at the hospital. "Were you not in that room? I've got nothing to offer you except a broken past, and a family trait of addiction."

My heart shatters into a millions pieces. "Do you really think that?"

He doesn't look at me, so I grab his face between my hands and pull his attention to me. "Nothing in there matters to me as much as the man in front of me. You are not your father and you never will be. I know you haven't been told this a lot in your lifetime, but there are people who love you, regardless of where you come from. I love you."

I freeze. *Did I just say that?*

I'm about to ask him to ignore that last part, but no. I want him to know. Even if he doesn't want me at the end of whatever this is, I want him to know that he is worthy of being loved.

"Lennox," his voice is rough and his eyes search mine for sincerity.

I drop my hands. "I just want you to know that you're never alone."

I turn and unlock my car, hoping he'll stop me. But he doesn't move. I back out of the parking lot, and he's still in the same spot.

I've waited for him for years. I can wait a little longer. Unless he doesn't feel the same way.

Then I just ruined everything.

Chapter 23

Lennox

I yawn as I open the front door of the house. It's almost eleven and my brothers are still here.

The rest of the employees are gone, but my brothers are helping mom clean up the house. The tables have been taken down, but the giant ice tree is still sitting in the back corner, slowly melting away. It's like watching the grinch "slowly" steal Christmas.

Sean is scrubbing floors, and Trent is cleaning tables, and Michael is doing the dishes. I feel like a kid again, when mom would make them pay for their consequences after misbehaving.

I smile. Then remind myself I'm supposed to be sad about my breakup with Noa.

Man, that feels like it was days ago.

All I can think about now is Grant. I want to be strong for him, but it didn't stop me from crying all the way home while Taylor Swift sang about one of her many past loves.

What if Grant doesn't believe me? What if he doesn't give me a chance to love him the way I want to?

"Oh Lennox," Juliet runs to me first and hugs me around the neck. She lowers her voice. "They totally believed it. Make them suffer." She shoots me a quick smile before letting go, and I muster up the remainder of my revenge for them.

"Lenny," Michael says, taking a hesitant step toward me, but I cut him off.

"My name is Lennox, and I'd like you to use it." I never hated the nickname, but I want them to see me as a woman and that won't happen as long as they keep calling me by the pet name I received as a baby.

My brothers look at me like I just sprouted wings. Maybe I have. I have to admit, I'm enjoying this.

"Are you okay?" Sean asks.

Something about the pitiful look in Sean's eyes, and the fact that I just made an unrequited declaration of love for Grant, gets me choked up, and I start sobbing.

All my brothers jump back like I have a disease.

I shake my head. "Emotions are not contagious. Would you idiots give me a hug and tell me I'm going to be okay?" I tell them.

They obey, and for the first time in my life, I get to enjoy a hug with all my brothers, without fear of slime being dumped down my back.

"What can we do?" Trent asks, and I assume it's him patting my back. He's always been the most sentimental.

I sniff and look up at each of my brothers, making sure they each get a good eyeful of my pain. "Noa and I were supposed to get matching tattoos tomorrow." I swipe at my tears. "I still want to do it. Will one of you do it with me?"

They shoot each other and me terrified looks, and it takes everything in me to not laugh.

"What?" Michael cracks first. "You want to get a tattoo?"

I start bawling, milking my tears for all their worth.

They begin arguing about who should do it with me. Trent votes Sean because he's always wanted a tattoo, but Sean is voting Michael because he's the oldest.

Two of them think they are getting out of it. But all three of them made the bet.

"Hey!" I look up at them. "Why don't we all get matching tattoos?"

Their jaws hang open so wide I can see how Sean's is still crooked from his motorcycle accident four years ago. And despite everything they've put me through, I love these guys to pieces.

"What?" Trent asks.

"Oh, what a nice sibling activity." My mom speaks up from the kitchen.

I laugh but cover it in time to make it look like I'm getting choked up.

Worried looks cover my brother's faces again and they rush to comfort me.

"Okay! We'll do it!" Sean pulls me in again and I smile into his chest.

"But it has to be small," Michael says.

"And tasteful." Trent begrudgingly agrees.

This time, the tears dripping down my cheeks are real. Noa was right. Their bets, while annoying and completely misguided, were their weird way of showing they love me.

Clearly, they could use more practice.

"Thank you!" I squeal and hug them all back. "The tattoo artist will be here tomorrow at ten."

Sean pulls back. "He's coming here?"

"She is." I smile. "She just started her own business, so she'll do them for free. Isn't that great?"

My brothers freeze, their eyes as wide as saucers

like I just gave them a death sentence.
Mission accomplished.

***

I can barely pull myself out of bed the next morning. I stayed up all night, waiting for Grant to text or call. Something. But every minute that ticks by without a word from him cuts into my heart a little more.

All night long, I distracted myself by thinking about this prank, so I didn't have to worry about Grant. But he's still the only thing on my mind. Even as I'm about to get a needle stuck in me that looks more like a syringe.

Yes, I had talked to Juliet's friend Karli about her help for this prank. And now I feel bad for saying I didn't like her. She understood her assignment.

"I don't think those needles are clean, Lennox," Trent says, halfway hiding behind me like Karli is a wild animal who might just rip his heart out.

Actually, she might.

"Sure they are," I say. "Right Karli?"

She gives me a dumbfounded look. "Are they supposed to be?"

"Yes, they're supposed to be!" Sean yells. Ever since Karli got here, my brothers have been nervously pacing the living room, though none of them will come right out and admit they're scared.

Revenge is so sweet.

"Fine," Karli grumbles. "So picky." She picks up the stack of needles and carries them into the kitchen.
How are the guys even buying this? What kind of tattoo artist carries around a box full of needles? I have no idea. Maybe they all do.

"Lennox." Michael turns to me as soon as she's out of sight. "I don't trust her. Let's maybe do this next year for Christmas, huh?"

    I paste on a frown. "I thought you were all willing to do this with me."

    "We are," Michael says quickly.

    "But not with this chick," Sean adds.

    "She'll kill us all," Trent says.

    She most definitely will. I keep this little tidbit of information to myself, though.

    "You big babies." Grandma hollers from the couch that she's been sitting on for the last hour, watching my brothers with glee. "A little tattoo is nothing to be afraid of. I can show you a real scar." She stands and turns around, reaching for her waistband.

    We all scream and turn away.

    "Man up." She cackles, and we wait a solid minute before turning back around so we glimpse something bound to scar us forever.

    Karli walks back into the living room with the same stack of needles. "They're as clean as they'll ever be."

    My brothers send me pleading looks, but I smile at Karli. "Michael wants to go first."

    Michael's eyes go wide and he reaches for his fiancé who is across the room. She ignores his pleas and takes a bite of a fresh cinnamon roll. "Ooh can ooh it," she cheers with her mouth full.

    Michael takes a deep breath and sits down on the folding chair we brought out just for the occasion.

    "At least it's not a bat this time, right?" He says to Karli.

    She glares at him and picks a needle, the biggest one apparently, and brings it to his ankle.

    He looks away from her and up at me. "I'm only doing this because I love you, Len."

My heart beats harder, and an overwhelming love fills my soul, and I can see the past in more clarity. Some of their pranks were just that. But the big ones that I thought I hated actually made me brave. I hated the soccer team, but I made my best friend on that team. The same friend who introduced me to graphic design. And the night I snuck out of my house with my friends was one of the best nights of my life. They used their bets to push me, because they loved me, not because they wanted to see me fail.

I lean over and wrap my arms around Michael. Who knew pulling this prank on them would teach *me* a lesson. "I love you too."

"Ow!" He jerks back and I barely catch myself from falling to the floor. "That hurt." He yells at Karli.

I look at Karli, my eyes wide. "What are you doing? You can't give people real tattoos."

"Chill." Karli smiles and holds up a tiny needle. "I just poked him with a pin."

"Wait." Michael jumps from the chair. "What's going on?"

"I think my work here is done." Karli stands but instead of leaving, she joins Juliet in the kitchen, snagging a cinnamon roll for herself.

"Lennox?" Michael scolds, "What was that?"

I look at each of them. Michael's unruly blond hair, Trent's baby cheeks that are covered with a neatly trimmed beard, and Sean's always innocent brown eyes.

"That, my brothers, was your payback for betting on my love life."

Their eyebrows furrow.

"What?" Sean yells.

"You guys never learn your lessons. So I decided

to help. I never even dated Noa." I smile. "He was just a friend pretending to be my fiancé for the night."

"No." Trent shakes his head and scratches his beard. "That was *all* a prank?"

I grin. It feels so good to beat them at their own game. "Sure was."

"Huh. Who knew little Lennox could pull one over on us all?" Michael shakes his head and looks at me with something akin to admiration.

I barely refrain from bowing.

Just kidding. I bowed.

"I guess she's learned a thing or two." Sean muses and he takes a step closer to me.

I immediately back up. Right into the couch.

"She still hasn't learned how to run away," Trent says, and then they all rush after me.

I don't have a fighting chance. They spray whipped cream on my face and tickle me until I can't breathe. But I've never felt so happy getting teased by my brothers.

Maybe these bets and pranks aren't too bad.

"What about Grant?" Michael asks as we take turns leaning over the kitchen sink, washing whipped cream out of our hair.

My hands freeze under the water. "What about him?"

"Did he know it was a bet?"

"He figured it out," I say, turning away and picking up a hand towel.

"Was he mad?"

I freeze, then slowly turn around to look at Michael. "Why would he be mad?"

"Because you pretended to be engaged to someone else while he's in love with you," Michael says, like he gives people this kind of news all the time.

"He didn't say that," I whisper. If he really loved me, then why didn't he say it back at the hospital? Why hasn't he texted, or called, or come home?

"But you love him too, don't you?" Michael asks. Last week, I would have denied it. But after last night, after that kiss, I can't.

"I do," I whisper.

"Dang," Michael shakes his head. "We've had a bet going on about you two for years. And we all lost."

"What?" I reel back.

Another bet? Of course, there was.

"What do you mean?"

He leans back against the counter, and that's when I notice my family watching me. Everyone. Even my grandma.

"We thought we could get Grant to admit it first," Michael says, and the usual joy from his bets isn't there. "So Juliet made another bet. She said you guys would be together by Christmas."

My mouth drops open and I shoot the traitor a glance. "What?"

She raises her hands. "If you can't beat 'em, join 'em?"

That sneaky little thing.

I shake my head. On second thought, she's going to fit in just fine.

"I promise I'll never make a bet again." Juliet hurries to say.

"Don't worry," I grin at Juliet, "you'll get what's coming." My smile falls. "But we're not together. So I guess, I'm the one who lost."

Pain fills my chest. *Why doesn't he feel the same?*

The room turns eerily quiet. Maybe I should have gotten a tetanus-infused tattoo. It would give me a different pain to focus on than the one consuming my heart.

"Eggnog anyone?" Grandma asks, completely misreading the room.

I sigh, pushing my tears back. My entire family is here. I should be enjoying every minute with them. Now that I like my brothers again. "I'd love some."

Chapter 24

Grant

There was a bet. Lennox almost got a tattoo, and she almost got her brothers to get one too.

I close out of the text thread with Trent.

Wow, I missed a lot in one day.

I push back in my chair and hit the wall. I forgot how small this kitchen is.

I scrub a hand down my face. I haven't talked to Lennox since the hospital two days ago. My dad was released, and I told myself I needed some time to be with him, but for the last thirty-six hours, I've done nothing but think about her.

"What's wrong?" My dad asks. He pushes away his plate. He barely ate any food.

I look up at him. He wasn't there for me for years, when all I needed was him. And I'm trying to get over that, but it's going to take some time. His prognosis isn't good. He has less than a year, but I'm hopeful we can mend our broken relationship. Maybe start building that bridge between two lost souls.

"The Bentley's made a bet about me and Lennox getting together."

He purses his lips. "You guys seemed happy at the hospital. I'm surprised you're upset about that."

I'm not upset about the bet. I'm upset with myself. Lennox told me she loved me, and I froze. I hadn't heard that word in so long; I didn't know how to respond. I've always loved Lennox, but her saying it out loud made it real. And I haven't had genuine love since my grandpa died.

"I didn't tell Lennox how I feel about her."

"Why not?"

"Because I'm scared..."

My dad picks up on what I'm not saying. "You're afraid she'll use that love to hurt you or leave you."

I shrug. "Maybe."

My father sighs, and his hand shakes around his glass as he raises it to his lips for a drink. "I didn't show you what love is, so it makes sense you'd be afraid. But if you've learned anything from me, it's that you can't learn anything from me."

I shake my head. "What?"

"Your mother and I only did one thing right, and that was you. But we gave up too easily when things got hard. We each had our own destructive ways of coping with hard things, but you were never that way." He coughs, then steadies his breathing. "Your grandpa taught you what I couldn't. He taught you to be brave."

My chest warms and I feel my grandpa right beside me. His comforting presence. Or maybe, for the first time, I feel comfortable with my father.

"Be brave, son." He pats my hand. "Give her everything I never gave you."

"I'll do my best."

I've already made that promise to myself and to her, whether she knows it or not. I want to give her everything. Starting with my love and ending with my last name.

Wow. I've been watching too many Hallmark

movies with the Bentleys.

**

The drive to the Bentley's house passes in a blur. It's Christmas Eve, and I know exactly where they'll be. They've probably just finished a dangerous round of Nerf wars and are now at the dining room table, yelling at each other over a very long and gruesome game of monopoly.

Lennox will get mad at her siblings soon and then offer to make them eggnog, or some other drink, which she'll destroy on purpose. They know what's coming and they will drink it anyway because they love her.

Knowing this, I sneak in the side door instead of knocking. I tiptoe into the kitchen and wait. Five minutes later, I hear someone yell, followed by soft footsteps.

I hide behind the door and wait until she's at the sink, then step out.

"Ah!" Grandma screams and clutches her chest. She staggers back toward the sink and I jump in to catch her before she falls.

"Mom!" Mark comes running into the kitchen, followed by everyone except Lennox.

"What happened?" Ms. B. asks Grandma.

Grandma narrows her eyes at me. "This little twit scared me." She hits my arm, then stops and rubs my bicep. "Nevermind, I forgive you."

I smile and make sure Grandma is steady before I release her.

"What are you doing in here?" Michael asks.

I scratch the back of my head. My brilliance was terribly misguided. "I was waiting for Lennox to come fix you guys a drink."

"She did that thirty minutes ago." Trent laughs. "Now she's crying in her room."

"What?" She's crying? "Why?"

Sean shrugs. "She lost UNO."

"Don't listen to those ninnies," Grandma says. "She says she's fine, but I know she's been waiting for you."

Something stabs me in the back. Quite literally, and I look at Grandma again.

Grandma glares. "Don't make her wait any longer, Muscles."

That's all the motivation I need.

I eagerly leave the kitchen and the seven pairs of judging eyes.

Every footstep down the hall feels heavier than the last. What if she's changed her mind about loving me? What if she's given up already?

I stand outside her door for at least five minutes. Why am I not moving?

"Really, Muscles?" Grandma appears beside me. "Do I have to do everything?" She raps on the door then waddles around the corner of the hall, where I suspect she'll stay for the next twenty to thirty minutes.

The door creaks open and my heart jumps out of my chest. Straight to her, where it's always belonged.

"Grant?"

She's beautiful. She's wearing sweats, and her hair and makeup aren't done. But there's nothing more attractive to me.

"Lennox." Her name rushes out of my mouth like a breath of fresh air.

I know her family is just down the hall, so I step inside her room and shut the door behind me. This puts us chest to chest and completely in the dark.

Perhaps I didn't think this one through either. I guess being in love doesn't give you all the answers.

"What are you doing?" She asks, and even in the dark, I know she's smiling.

"I'm here to fix the mistake I made two days ago by not telling you something," I say.

"Oh," she breathes. "Should I turn on the light?"

"I'll tell you either way and then kiss you regardless, so it's your choice," I say fervently.

"In that case..." Her hand finds mine instead of the light switch and I fall a little more in love with her.

"I didn't have a loving family like you did." I start. "So I lied to you guys. I was terrified that if anyone ever found out my deep dark secrets, I'd be rejected from the only family I've ever really known."

"But Grant—"

"Shh, sweetheart, I know. I should have been smart enough to see that your family would never reject me. That *you* would never reject me."

She lifts a hand to my chest, and while I'm quite happy with where this is going, I'm not finished yet.

I cover her hand with mine.

"That's why I never told you how I felt. I feared that if you didn't feel the same, I wouldn't be able to come around anymore. So when you told me you loved me, I freaked out. I haven't heard those words since I was fourteen, and they meant so much more coming from you. You're the most important person in the world to me and I want to make you happy. But I had to be sure I wouldn't screw this up first."

"Grant," she whispers. "Everyone screws up. The only thing that matters is that we keep trying."

My eyes burn, and for once, I let the tears fall without a battle. "This tattoo on my chest was the promise I made to myself, and to you, to be the man you deserved." I slide a hand up her arm and tangle it in her hair. "I love you, Lennox Bentley."

I feel her lean in, feel myself close the distance, and then—

"He said it! He said he loved her!" Someone hollers on the other side of the door.

"I'm going to kill them." Lennox tries to pull out of my arms, but I pull her right back.

"We'll kill them together. Later. There's something more important I want to do right now."

I find her lips in the darkness, and my entire world lights up. Her lips are soft and taste like vanilla and hope. I want her in my life. Always and forever. I do. Or whatever it is. Whatever promise I have to make to keep her, I will.

She threads her fingers through my hair, deepening the kiss, deepening my love for her.

When she pulls back, a growl escapes my throat.

"Oh, I almost forgot. I have a present for you," she says and flips on the lights.

My eyes take a moment to adjust to the room and when they do, she's handing me something.

A sturdy, wooden chest. The chest I gave her.

I run my fingers over the carved wooden lid, the same symbol on my chest.

"I know yours burned, so I figured we could share mine." She bites her bottom lip.

I want to cry, but I've done enough of that for the foreseeable future. So I school my features into a solemn frown. "You're re-gifting me your old things," I say.

Her eyes go wide. "What? No— I... You lost your grandpa's I..." She covers her mouth with her hand, but it doesn't stop me from seeing the red creep into her cheeks.

I pry her hand away from her mouth. She should never hide such a thing of beauty. "I'm kidding. I love it. Thank you."

She smiles that soft sweet smile that has always had me rolling over like a puppy and begging for more.

She plays with the collar of my shirt, and I shiver when her fingernail tickles my skin. She goes up on her tiptoes and I drop my head, but she turns my face to the side and puts her lips near my ear.

"Will you still love me if I say, you owe me a hundred dollars?"

I scratch my head, confused, before it hits me. But she's already sprinting out of the room.

"I'm not giving you money for dating another man," I holler, chasing after her.

Everyone is in the family room, and I don't even care. When I catch Lennox there, I give her a kiss, long and hard, to the cheers of our audience. They wanted it. They got it.

Someone clears their throat. "Hey, maybe not so close to the Christmas tree, guys."

Epilogue

Grant

Three months later

"I bet you twenty bucks she's wearing tennis shoes so she can take off before making it down the aisle," Sean whispers in my ear.

I casually elbow him in the gut, and he groans. This is my wedding; I can't really take him out right now.

My wedding. I never thought I'd say that. I also never thought I'd be waiting for Lennox to walk down that aisle. We only dated a month before getting engaged. Why wait when all we've ever wanted was each other?

I look out at the crowd. Everyone I have ever loved and cared about is here. Even my dad. He is doing better for now, and I'm enjoying getting to know the man I always wished for while growing up.

Lennox and I closed on our house a month ago and we filled it with things we picked out together. We made it our home. And now when I go home, I know I won't be alone anymore. Because she's there. She's my home.

But where is she now?

I send her a text.

Me: Where are you? *Picture me not so patiently waiting*

Lennox: Carb Loading.

It's followed by a picture of her sticking a giant piece of pizza in her mouth.

I laugh out loud, then realize I'm in the front of a church and step behind my groomsmen. One of them being Noa. I've decided he's not too bad. Even if he tried to drug me once.

Me: Bring me some?
Lennox: I'll be the girl carrying pizza instead of a bouquet.
Me: Flowers are overrated.

I step back out to my assigned spot. The wedding March starts, and my pulse picks up. Why is it such a slow song? With as fast as my heart is racing, it should be something heavy metal.

A curtain parts in the back of the room, and out steps Lennox. Her dress hugs her beautiful figure, then flares out just below her hips, but it's not her figure I'm looking at now. All I see are her bright, beautiful eyes. The eyes that show me every day how much she loves me, with just a look. I vow to myself and to her at this moment that I will never do anything to take away that light.

"Take care of her son," Mark says, handing over my fiancée.

"Always," I whisper, pulling her close to my side.

"Did my brothers make any bets?" Lennox asks as we take our places.

"Only about twenty-five," I say.

"Let's give them a show then." She grins and then she kisses me. We haven't even made it through the first sentence, and we're already kissing.

Looks like I won.

The End

Thank you!

I can't explain how much I loved writing Grant and Lennox's story. Their story came so easy, and while I wrote, all I thought about was you, the reader! Thank you for taking a chance on this little novella. I hope you loved these characters as much as I do!

Reviews help so much, and if you can, consider rating on Amazon, Goodreads, or Bookbub.

Connect with me on Instagram @authorjenessafayeth

Wait!

Didn't get enough of Grant and Lennox? Don't worry, I've got you. Sign up for my newsletter to recieve an EXTRA epilogue. You don't want to miss this :)

https://dashboard.bookfunnel.com/books/273101/giveaways/new?signup=required

*This link will also be available in the bio on my Instagram page.

Acknowledgements

I would like to thank Brynlee, for completing this bet in real life, and inspiring this story. Also, thank you for not pretending to be engaged.

Thank you to Rebekah Goodman, for boosting my spirits when I was about ready to toss this whole thing in the trash.

Thank you to my beta readers who blew my mind with all their love and support!

A huge thank you to my Aunt Jill who patiently explains everything to me at least fifty times until I get it.

About The Author

Jenessa Fayeth

Jenessa Fayeth doesn't remember the last time she got a full night's sleep, but she does know how late she can stay up reading to survive the next day. In college she majored in Family Life and Human Development, and she now uses that knowledge to convince herself she isn't crazy while raising her wild children. Her hobbies include reading, writing, sleeping and eating. She writes all night and is a mom and wife all day. She is constantly exhausted, but she wouldn't change it for the world.

Books In This Series

Just A Bentley Christmas

Four Bentleys. Four Christmases. It only gets crazier every year.

Just A Date

Juliet:

I've been relegated to my best friend's "psych project". Talk about an ego booster. She thinks I need love in my life but if my parent's divorce taught me anything, it is that I absolutely don't. I'd rather stick with math. Numbers are safer than feelings. But no matter how hard I try I can't just think of Michael as a number.

Michael

I never thought I'd be locked in a bet in order to get a promotion at my family business. Blame it on stupidity, or my brother, (technically he's both). The bet is simple: fall in love in thirty days. But the girl capturing my heart has sworn off dating. I'll have to get creative.

Books By This Author

Chasing Him

Addison Spencer has crazy dreams. The craziest? An idealized relationship with the popular and ridiculously handsome Dean Hunter.But Addie also dreams of being a writer. Thanks to her best friend, and a nosy college advisor, she finds herself chasing both dreams at once. Her task? Follow ten easy steps to win Dean's heart, and then, oh yeah, write about it for the school paper.Every author needs a good story. But is that all this project will be? Or is it possible for a girl like Addie to catch Dean Hunter? If only she were the only one chasing him.

Choosing Him

Addison Spencer did the impossible. She landed the boy of her dreams while writing about it for the high school paper. But happily ever afters aren't always what they are cracked up to be. She's been dutifully waiting seven months for her boyfriend, Dean, to return from Mexico. But the flirt in her science class won't leave her alone. Chase is funny and charming and out of his mind if he thinks he can catch Addie's attention. But to Addie's dismay, he does just that. It doesn't help that communication with Dean has been all but nonexistent and some of her greatest fears have become a reality. Dean's unexpected return is far from a fairytale ending, and Addie finds herself caught between two men who care for her. How does she make her heart choose? Happily ever after isn't always an easy choice.

If It's You

You can't win a war by falling for the enemy.

Christian wanted nothing more than a relaxing summer to forget about the loss he'd experienced at home. But the farm is anything but relaxing, and the farmers beautiful daughter is determined to send him packing before he even makes it a week. But he needs a distraction, and teasing her seems to be the perfect way to keep his mind off of his life. It's a harmless game, because he'd never fall for a girl like her.

Maizie is no stranger to pain. Which is exactly what this handsome city boy is: a pain in her rear. She could've gotten over the embarrassment of their first meeting if he didn't seem so hell-bent on ruining her life. Two can play that game, though, and she's determined to win, even if it means losing something even more important.

Manufactured by Amazon.ca
Bolton, ON